"I'LL SCREAM IF YOU DON'T LET ME GO," Kathleen promised.

He wrote in her palm in bold, angry strokes.

Scream.

Memories threatened her once more. The last time she'd threatened to scream, they'd ended up on the ground together, joined body, heart, and soul.

She felt the heat of Hunter's body and his warm breath against her cheek. He was so close. . . .

"Why did you have to find me?" she whispered.

He cupped her face. His hands were exquisitely tender as he traced her eyebrows, her cheekbones, her lips. She knew he was going to kiss her; she felt it in the way he held his body, the way he touched her skin.

And she knew she was going to let him. Because she had to. Because she would not be able to live if she didn't feel his lips on hers once more. . . .

WHAT ARE *LOVESWEPT* ROMANCES?

They are stories of true romance and touching emotion. We believe those two very important ingredients are constants in our highly sensual and very believable stories in the LOVESWEPT *line. Our goal is to give you, the reader, stories of consistently high quality that may sometimes make you laugh, sometimes make you cry, but are always fresh and creative and contain many delightful surprises within their pages.*

Most romance fans read an enormous number of books. Those they truly love, they keep. Others may be traded with friends and soon forgotten. We hope that each LOVESWEPT *romance will be a treasure—a "keeper." We will always try to publish*

LOVE STORIES YOU'LL NEVER FORGET BY AUTHORS YOU'LL ALWAYS REMEMBER

The Editors

Loveswept

709

ONLY HIS TOUCH

PEGGY WEBB

BANTAM BOOKS
NEW YORK · TORONTO · LONDON · SYDNEY · AUCKLAND

ONLY HIS TOUCH

A Bantam Book / September 1994

Bantam Books are published by Bantam Books, a division of Bantam Dou-
bleday Dell Publishing Group, Inc. Its trademark, consisting of the words
"Bantam Books" and the portrayal of a rooster, is Registered in U.S.
Patent and Trademark Office and in other countries. Marca Registrada.
Bantam Books, 1540 Broadway, New York, New York 10036.

PRINTED IN THE UNITED STATES OF AMERICA

OPM   0 9 8 7 6 5 4 3 2 1

This book is for my nephew,
Seth Fortune,
in celebration of his high-school graduation.

I owe a special debt of gratitude to my dear friend Reverend George Cantin, Oxford, Mississippi, whose beautiful spirit transcends his blindness. Also, I want to thank Sarah Karrant, Ballet Studio, Tupelo, Mississippi, whose exquisite beauty graces the cover of this novel.

PROLOGUE

Six years was too long to live a lie. Standing at the railing with her back to the sea, Kathleen Shaw watched her husband cross the teakwood deck. His generous smile would have broken her heart if she'd had a heart to break.

When he got close enough, he slid his arm around her and leaned down to kiss her cheek.

"I don't know which is more breathtaking, darling, you or the sea. No wonder you spend so much time up here."

"The water is peaceful, Earl."

He pulled her close, and she leaned against him, unconsciously reaching for the gold locket that nestled between her breasts.

"Enjoy it while it lasts. We'll be docking at Cape Town tomorrow, and you'll be the belle of a social whirl that will make Mardi Gras seem tame."

"You're the one who will cause the stir, Doctor."

"My Kathleen. Always sweet and sassy." He kissed her on the tip of her nose. "Are you ready for dinner, darling?"

"You go ahead. I'll be down in a while."

"Don't take too long. Time drags when you're not at my side."

She blew him a kiss, and he caught it in his left hand and pressed it to his lips. Dr. Earl Lennox, brilliant scientist, great humanitarian, adoring husband. How could she ever tell him good-bye without destroying him?

As soon as he was out of sight, she hurried to their cabin and got a small silver box that was buried underneath her lingerie. Just holding the box felt like a betrayal of her husband. He would be sipping a glass of wine now, probably smiling, expecting at any moment to see her slip through the door and take her place at his side.

Her hands trembled as she pressed the spring on her gold locket and took out a tiny key. Opening the box, she took out the contents, a stack of letters yellow with age.

She was shivering now with the need to see the words that had sustained her for so many years, but she couldn't bear to read them in the room she shared with her husband, in view of the bed where they had made sedate, gentle love. With the letters pressed close to her heart, she hurried topside. The moon was out and the water had turned to pewter.

Leaning against the railing, she opened the first letter and began to read: *Kat, Even as I write I can feel you lying naked in my arms. I can see the pattern the sun makes on your skin as it comes down through the Spanish moss. Here is my heart, love. Wear it next to yours until I come again. Hunter.*

She'd worn the locket over her heart and waited for him, waited seven long years. At first she could track his quest for his father through his letters. Then the letters had stopped.

And when he finally had come, it had been too late.

She unsnapped the locket and looked at the photograph—Hunter at eighteen, with his untamed black hair blown even wilder by the ride on the ferris wheel, his arm thrown carelessly across her shoulders as if he had no need to hold her closer, as if he knew she would always be his. How they had laughed when they crowded together in the cheap booth at the carnival and posed for the photograph. Then, afterward, in the heated closeness with the tinkling music of the carousel coming through the curtain, they looked at each other and their laughter died.

"*Kat,*" he whispered with his cheek against hers. "*Will you love me forever?*"

"*Yes. Forever.*"

His kiss set them off on a journey of frantic

exploration. A security guard had threatened to call the cops if they didn't come out.

Slowly Kathleen closed the locket. A breeze from the Atlantic ruffled her hair and cooled her hot cheeks. She carefully refolded the letter and slipped it into her pocket; then, turning, she looked out across the sea. Somewhere in the distance was Africa. And deep in its dark heart was Hunter La Farge.

Belowdecks her husband would be glancing at his watch, wondering what was taking her so long and trying to decide whether to start the first course without her. If she didn't go down soon, he would come up to look for her.

She took one last, longing look across the water, and then she turned her back on the sea and started below to her husband.

The first explosion tilted the deck and knocked her back against the railing. The second spewed fire into the night sky.

"Hunter!" Kathleen screamed.

And then she was sucked into the center of the holocaust.

ONE

The boat slid quietly through the waters of the Zambezi. The only sounds were the hushed whisper of oars and the click of the camera. With the grace of the jungle cats he often photographed, Hunter stood up in the boat, hardly causing it to sway.

"Someday you're going to do that and we'll both fall in and be eaten by a crocodile," Rick said.

Loyal from the top of his flaming red hair down to the tips of his elevated cowboy boots, Rick Ransom would do anything for his boyhood friend except be eaten by something that swam, flew, or stalked through the jungles. He'd left a comfortable home and an easy life in Jefferson Parish to follow Hunter La Farge all over South Africa in pursuit of diamonds, and regretted it only in times of danger. Which was more often than he cared to think about. Why Hunter felt compelled to leave his tightly guarded estate in Johannesburg to trek all over the jungles for months at a time was beyond him.

"Any crocodile worth his salt would run screaming at the sight of me." Hunter braced his feet and took aim with his camera.

"That's the truth. What I don't understand is why the women don't do the same thing?"

"Women love nothing better than trying to tame something wild."

"Maybe I ought to grow a beard too."

Hunter's hearty laugh boomed across the water, sending a flock of birds into flight. "You'd still look like a boy scout. No, Rick, I think you should leave all the women to me and stick to escorting old ladies across the street."

"Just for that I ought to dump you in with the crocs."

"Then how would you get back to Johannesburg?"

"My charm, maybe?"

They fell into an easy silence, and when they docked, Hunter's Baron was serviced and ready to fly. He geared up and slid into the cockpit.

"Home, here we come," he said.

"You call this hellhole home? Home is a front porch under the live-oak trees, a tall mint julep, and a long-stemmed Louisiana beauty at my beck and call."

"You can have Jefferson Parish. I find hell more to my liking."

Hunter set the plane down on his sprawling private compound that held a landing strip, a house that looked as if it had sprung up naturally among the trees and exotic flowering vines, and the offices of La Farge Diamond Company. The first thing he did was go to his office and plow through the backlog of newspapers.

With the papers towering between them, he and Rick began to read, gleaning information pertinent to the diamond market and the political climate of the nation they now called home.

"Listen to this," Rick said. " 'Yacht explosion off the coast of Cape Town claims lives of—' "

Rick stopped reading, and a silence like death fell on the room. Suddenly chilled to the bone, Hunter reached across the stack and took the paper out of Rick's hand. The item was headline news.

" 'Yacht explosion off the coast of Cape Town claims lives of scientist Earl Lennox and famed prima ballerina Kathleen Shaw.' "

Hunter forced his hands not to shake, forced himself to sit still while he continued reading.

" 'Best known for her roles as Aurora in *Sleeping Beauty* and Odette/Odile in *Swan Lake*, Ms. Shaw was accompanying her husband, who was scheduled to deliver a paper on AIDS to a conference of colleagues in Cape Town.' "

He looked at the paper's date. Kathleen had been dead three months and he hadn't known.

"This is wrong," he said.

"Here's another. . . . 'Search for the bodies of Kathleen Shaw and her husband, Dr. Earl Lennox, has been called off. All who were aboard the yacht are believed to be dead. . . .'" Rick turned to look at Hunter. "It's dated six weeks after the one you have."

Hunter folded the paper, tucked it under his arm, and started toward the door.

"Where are you going?" Rick said.

"I have to know if she's dead."

The pale sliver of a moon looked as if it had been thrown carelessly into the sky and had snagged itself on the topmost branches of a massive live-oak tree. Standing at the window of a small cottage nearby, Hunter stared at the tree. A breeze off the Mississippi stirred the Spanish moss that dripped from its branches and brushed the ground. Hunter watched the shadowy dance of the moss.

Suddenly he grabbed the windowsill, gripping it so hard, his knuckles turned white. The moss swayed in the breeze, and inside its lacy curtain, another shadow moved.

"Kat," he whispered.

A pale glimmer of moonlight fell on a filmy white skirt, and a whisper of wind lifted it like a bird. Groaning, Hunter pressed his hands to his eyes and bent his head.

"I must be going mad."

When he looked at the tree once more, the phantom had disappeared. Shaken by his vision, he went into the kitchen and made himself a stiff drink.

"This is what comes of chasing a dream," he said. "Insanity."

His hands shook as he lifted the drink to his lips. For six months he'd combed the ocean, searching for Kathleen Shaw's body. And now when'd he come back to Jefferson Parish to bid her good-bye, his weary mind had conjured her up, waiting for him under the oak tree just as she had when she was sixteen.

He finished his drink, then fell into his bed, exhausted. Sleep claimed him quickly, and with it came the phantom of the oak tree, tossing her long gypsy hair and teasing him with her full red lips.

"Do I kiss better than anybody you know, Hunter?"

"You're the only girl I've ever kissed, Kat."

"I would be furious if you'd said yes."

"Then I would have kissed you until you lost your breath and forgot your question."

"Kiss me until I lose my breath."

Her lips were ripe as berries, and when she parted them, he thrust his tongue inside, tasting all her sweetness until he was drunk with her. Reeling, he propped one hand against the tree trunk and gazed down at her. Her face was a perfect heart in the moonlight, framed by her lustrous black hair.

"If I don't stop now, I won't be able to," he said.

"Don't stop." She wove her hands into his hair and pulled him closer. "Oh, please. Don't stop."

"Do you know what you're asking, Kat?"

"Hunter La Farge, do you take me for a fool? I know exactly what I'm asking." She tightened her grip in his hair until his scalp hurt. "I've loved you since I was five years old, and if you don't relieve me of the burden of my virginity right this very minute, I'm going to start screaming."

He laughed, loving her so much, he was hurting with it.

"You'll wake the neighbors, and they'll all come pouring out of their houses asking what's going on. Then what will you do?"

"I'll say I saw a snake and you refused to kill it. And then you'll be branded as a coward."

"I'm no coward, Kat."

"I know." She slid her hand inside his shirt, and his skin caught fire. "Are you going to kill that snake, or what?"

"This is blackmail, you know."

"I know." Her hands were white as lilies as she unbuttoned her blouse and shucked her jeans. Exposed, she stood before him, her skin as creamy and soft as the gardenias that perfumed the sultry air. She cupped her breasts and lifted them in innocent seduction. "I'm yours, Hunter."

"You've always been mine . . . even before we were born."

How he knew those things, he couldn't say. All he knew was the certainty he felt when he touched her silky skin, the joy he felt when he kissed her satiny lips. Fear that he would fail her never entered his mind. She lay beneath him on the soft ground, offered up to him like the tender bud of a rose.

Slick rain-drenched leaves swayed in the night breeze and sprayed droplets of water across her skin. Bending over her like some fine animal from an exotic faraway place, Hunter licked the moisture away, licked with slow, sweeping movements as if he were absorbing her through his tongue, branding himself forever with the feel and taste of her skin.

The moon dropped down to the top of their private tree, and a drop of moisture on her nipple caught the light and sent it, prismlike, bursting into a thousand colors that blinded him. He caught the prism between his lips and carried it deep into himself, where it exploded, brilliant as a comet.

Bright with her colors, he entered her, seeking to take possession. And buried deep in her, he found himself possessed. Her cry was one of pure primitive pleasure, and when she began to move beneath him, it was with a certainty and a fluidity that said more clearly than words that she was where she belonged and that she'd waited all her life for this moment.

With the vigor of youth and none of its awkwardness, they rode the waves of passion until the moon paled and the stars fell from the sky, rode until *they entered a dimension of their own making, a place beyond time and space where nothing existed except the two of them and their love, forged over the years and finally given form by their simple act of trust.*

Again and again he poured himself into her, and when finally he lay back, slick with sweat and carrying her scent upon his skin, she lifted herself on her elbows and gazed into his eyes, far back where he carried his secrets.

"Oh, Hunter . . . I am lost." She pressed one hand over her breast and the other over his heart. "Don't you feel it? We've traded places. You are me and I am you. We're the same person, Hunter."

"I've always known that. I carry your soul and you carry mine." He pulled her down to him, and her hair curtained their faces. "We're one, Kat. Now and forever."

He positioned her hips over his and once more began that long, silken slide to oblivion.

"Kat . . . Kat . . ."

Hunter woke himself up calling her name. Sweat covered his body, and the damp sheets were twisted around his legs. He reached out to the other side of the bed, half expecting to find her there, her black hair fanned across the pillow, tangled from their lovemaking and gleaming in the moonlight.

"Kat," he whispered, and the sound of his own groaning mocked him.

Damning her soul to black everlasting hell

for marrying someone else while he was gone off trying to find a father whose name he didn't even know, Hunter went into the bathroom and turned on the light. He looked like something that had been dragged through the jungle. He splashed water over his face, then stuck his head under the faucet and stood while water saturated his hair.

Even then, he couldn't get cool.

Calling himself every kind of fool, he slipped outside and hurried to the oak tree. Her fragrance lingered there, caught in the moss that swayed in the river breezes like a lace curtain. Riveted, he closed his eyes and inhaled deeply. He was being foolishly romantic, of course. The perfume that sent his senses reeling was not Kat's, but belonged to the gardenias that bloomed against the fence.

Nevertheless, he knelt and studied the ground, trying to see footprints in the dark.

There . . . Was that the imprint of her foot? That dainty curving indention in the moss?

He pressed his hand over the imprint. His body pulsed with heat, as if he'd stuck his finger into an electrical outlet. A breeze caught the leaves, and they seemed to whisper her name.

Dark clouds that had been hovering off the coast moved inland and dumped their contents on the parched earth. The tree protected Hunter for a while, and then even its thick branches couldn't keep the onslaught away. Thunder crashed and lightning splintered the skies.

Hunter lifted his fists and cursed the rain. He cursed every drop of water that had ever dared to fall. If there had been no water, there would have been no ocean. And if there were no ocean, Kathleen would not be lying in a watery grave.

At last, drenched, wretched, and haunted, he made his way back to the house. Pulling a chair close to the window, he sat down and stared into the dark at the tree.

TWO

As soon as it was daylight, Hunter walked the city, revisiting all the places that held her memory—the bend in the river where she'd sat on the stone wall and told him he would be king of the world; the streetcar she used to ride up and down St. Charles, pointing out the grand houses where she would go for tea when she became famous; the cathedral where she'd stood in white satin and pledged her love to another man.

And finally the tree.

Just after dark when the fireflies began their dance of lights, Hunter returned to the live-oak tree that guarded the two tiny cottages where they'd grown up. Hunter La Farge and Kathleen Shaw, poor white trash with last names their mothers had made up. From the time Hunter had rescued her from the tree where she was throwing stones at the children calling her a *bastard*, they'd stood two against the world.

He stood underneath the tree with the moss touching his face and fireflies lighting the branches like tiny Christmas-tree bulbs.

"Good-bye, Kathleen," he said. "Good-bye, my love."

The leaves whispered in the wind, a ghost voice bidding him farewell.

Inside the cottage, he propped his hips against the faded Formica countertop and telephoned Rick to get a report on his diamond mines.

"The mines in the Transvaal are producing like Aladdin's Cave," Rick said. "We're going to be obscenely rich."

"I'm already obscenely rich." *And I'd give every penny I have for one glimpse of Kathleen.*

"You don't sound good, Hunter. When are you coming back?"

"I don't know."

"Don't take too long, buddy. It's dull out here on the dark continent without you. I haven't been threatened by a croc since you left."

A shadow moved under the oak tree. Riveted, Hunter stared out the window. Behind the curtain of moss was the silhouette of a woman with her arms outstretched. In the moonlight her hands shone as white as lilies.

"Hunter?" Rick said. "Are you there?"

The phone dangled from its cord as Hunter bolted toward the door. If he was going to be visited by a phantom, he was going to confront it, face-to-face.

He approached the tree cautiously, afraid that noise and haste would make the vision disappear. As he moved closer he saw the lithe outline of a woman's body. She was dressed in black and her face was hidden by a dark veil.

She stood unmoving, her head tilted to one side, her hands nestled against her breasts like two snow-white doves.

Hunter could hardly breathe. He was so close to her now that the moss brushed against his cheeks. Still, she didn't move.

"Are you a vision from heaven or a vision from hell?" he said.

There was no answer. A sultry fragrance perfumed the air, and he knew it was too rich and too close to be the gardenias.

He reached his hand through the mossy curtain, still half-afraid that the woman would prove to be a phantom.

"Who's there?"

With his hand in the air, Hunter froze. The voice, deep and sultry, came from behind the black veil.

"Kathleen?" Hunter whispered.

She reached out slowly, and when she took her hands away from her breasts, a shaft of moonlight pierced the thick leaves and fell on the gold locket resting against her soft, creamy skin.

Shock almost sent Hunter to his knees. It was the locket he'd left in the knothole of the tree thirteen years earlier right before he'd climbed aboard the freighter going to Africa. His farewell gift to Kathleen. His pledge that he would return to claim her.

But it couldn't be. She was dead.

The moon shuffled behind a cloud once more, and they were left alone in the velvet darkness.

"Is someone there?" she said. It was Kathleen's voice he heard, Kathleen's hands he saw reaching toward him.

"Don't you know me, Kathleen? Don't you remember?"

She took a step forward then, her hand stretched out in front of her. It grazed the mossy curtain, two inches from the place where his own hand hovered.

"Is anyone there?"

Even in the dark with the veil over her face, she should have seen him. Standing so close, she should have heard him.

The truth hit Hunter with the force of an explosion, and he doubled his hands into fists and shook them at the uncaring sky. Kathleen stood on the other side of the lacy Spanish moss, the gold locket shining against her cleavage.

The locket drew him like a beacon, and he

reached out, his hand hovering so close, his fingertips almost skimmed her satiny skin. She tipped her head back, and behind the veil, her eyes stared straight into his.

"Kat," he whispered. "Kat."

She neither saw nor heard.

Silently cursing himself, he drew his hand back. He didn't dare touch her, not in the dark while she was alone under the tree. She would be terrified.

She sighed, the sound as soft as wind through the leaves, then stepped back until she could touch the trunk of the tree.

"I must have been dreaming," she said. And then she turned around and left the live oak with small, even steps, counting under her breath as she walked.

Hunter watched until she was across the yard and through the door of the tiny cottage where she'd been born; then he leaned his face against the rough bark of the tree. Her fragrance and the warmth of her hand still lingered there.

He closed his eyes, and down the corridors of the past came her laughter, as clear as bells.

"Listen, Hunter? Do you hear the music?" She *lifted her arms and twirled around and around the tree. "I'm going to dance forever."* Dropping beside

him on the grass, she covered his face with kisses.
"Oh, Hunter. Don't ever let the music stop for me."

Hunter's shoulders shook as he cried without sound. He'd let the music stop for Kathleen. How would she ever forgive him?

Kathleen felt the presence of the cottage before she got to the door. Resisting the urge to hold her hands out in front of her, she counted the remaining steps to the entrance.

Exactly four. And the door was where it was supposed to be.

Triumphant, she pushed it open and marched inside.

"I did it, Martha. I did it without a cane."

Martha smelled like bath talcum and the tart lemony soap she used. Her large, solid hand caught Kathleen's and squeezed her encouragement.

Kathleen took off her hat and hung it on the peg beside the door, then made her way to the table and sat in a straight-backed chair. She tried to move with the slow grace of a ballerina instead of the slow uncertainty of the blind. Sometimes, when she was tempted to curse the darkness, she remembered the final darkness that had claimed her husband, and she knew that being alive was a miracle.

It wasn't the darkness that bothered her most, but the silence.

"Is the music playing, Martha?"

Martha squeezed her hand once. *Yes.*

"You won't let it stop, will you?"

Two squeezes of the large, capable hand. *No.*

Kathleen held herself very still, and she imagined she felt the beat of the music vibrating the old wooden floor and coming through the soles of her feet.

"Martha, I had the strangest feeling at the tree tonight." Silence swirled around her, and she pictured the other woman leaning forward, perhaps puzzled by the mysteries of Kathleen's mind. Martha was a nurse, practical as a pair of rain boots, and just as sturdy.

"I felt Hunter there with me."

The silence beat through her, and then she felt the glass that was pressed into her hand. Warm milk. It was Martha's cure for everything.

"Are you going to make me drink this?"

One tap on the back of her hand. *Yes.*

Kathleen shoved the glass aside and ran her hands through her hair. It felt heavy and glossy. At least she still had her hair. And her arms and legs.

"Hunter was so real to me tonight that I felt his hands on my breast."

She shivered at the memory. The presence she'd sensed in the dark had the power of gravity, drawing her out of herself, so that she felt as if she were trapped inside Hunter's skin with his heart beating against her chest and his blood flowing through her veins. With the old wildness filling her, she'd flown free of the silent darkness and had tumbled headlong into the world of stunning color and heat and light that they'd visited so many years ago.

Even now, sitting on the hard chair in the small kitchen with the old smells of rusty faucets and molding linoleum, she still carried a part of that private world with her, still felt the heat rushing through her blood.

Impossible dreams, now. Impossible love.

"I'm glad it was only my imagination," she said. "I'd rather die than have Hunter see me like this."

Martha pressed the glass back into her hand, then tapped it twice, harder this time. Smiling, Kathleen picked up the warm milk.

"You're a tyrant, Martha."

Kathleen drank the milk, then pushed back her chair.

"I'll be in my studio. And Martha . . . tell the president I'm not to be disturbed, and decline all invitations from England's queen."

She hoped Martha laughed. Laughter was certainly better than tears.

The president wouldn't be calling, of course, nor the queen. Both of them thought she was dead. And that's exactly how Kathleen wanted it, at least for a while.

She had no intention of being an object of pity. She'd stay dead until she could grace the stage once more, not as a blind ballerina but as the prima ballerina she'd worked so hard to become.

Because she wasn't concentrating, she walked smack into a wall.

"Damn." She put out her hands to reorient herself. The doorway to her studio was three steps to her right, and when she was inside, she walked the perimeter, holding on to the walls and counting the steps. It wasn't grand like the one in her flat in New York and the ones Earl had built for her in their houses in Charleston and Paris. But it was full of memories.

When she'd first discovered her love of and talent for dance, she and her mother had knocked down the wall between Kathleen's bedroom and the dining room, then sold all the furniture in those two rooms except the bed in order to buy mirrors and a ballet barre.

After the room was finished, Karen Shaw had cupped her daughter's face with her work-roughened hands and said, "You're going to be the grandest ballerina of them all. Just you wait and see."

The mirrors were gone now. Martha had taken them down so Kathleen wouldn't crash into the glass and cut herself.

She went to the small cabinet that held her collection of CDs and ran her hands over the braille labels. Tchaikovsky. Tonight she would reprise her greatest role. When the CD was in place, Kathleen counted steps to the center of the studio and stood very still, trying to feel the vibration of the music through the soles of her feet and the pores of her skin.

There was nothing except silence.

She went back to the sound system and ran her hands lightly along the front until she felt the knob that controlled volume. When she turned it up, she felt the first vibrations of music through her arms.

"I'm going to do it," she said. "Just you wait and see."

Sinking to the floor, she put on her ballet shoes.

Hunter heard the music coming from Kathleen's house. *Swan Lake.* He'd seen her dance Odette/Odile in Paris, sitting at the back of the opera house with his glasses trained on center stage. She hadn't even known he was there.

Except for a small light in the kitchen, her house was dark. The music came from Kathleen's studio. He and Karen Shaw used to sit cross-legged on the floor and applaud while Kathleen spun around in the sun.

My very own spotlight, she'd say. *Look. I'm dancing*.

There was no sun now, no spotlight. Only darkness and the music.

Leaving the tree, he crossed the yard that

separated their houses until he was standing just outside the pool of light pouring from the kitchen window. Every fiber in his body vibrated with the need to rush into her house, take Kathleen in his arms, and never let go. But it was very late . . . perhaps thirteen years too late.

He stood in the darkness and strained his eyes toward her studio window. At first he could see nothing, but gradually he made out her shadow, barely visible in the faint light that filtered down the hall from the kitchen and the small glow of the sound system. As his eyes adjusted to the darkness the shadow became more distinct.

"My God. She's dancing."

Kathleen spun around the room, not in time to the music, but two beats behind, like a graceful shadow hurrying to catch its owner. Suddenly she wobbled. Hunter caught his breath. Kathleen's arms fought the air until she had her balance, then she spun away once more.

And went crashing into the wall.

Tense, Hunter rushed to help her and was halfway to her kitchen door before he stopped himself.

"Fool. Do you think she wants your help now?"

Through the window he saw Kathleen slump her shoulders and bow her head, a picture of total defeat.

"Come on . . . come on," he whispered. "You can do it."

As if she'd heard, she straightened her shoulders and walked back to the center of the room. Then, with arms lifted and chin up, she leaped into the air once more.

Her landing was solid. In the darkness Hunter silently applauded.

"*Brava*, Kathleen. *Brava*."

With dizzying speed she spun around the room . . . once, twice. Then she toppled like a tower of cards, vanishing from his view. Hunter clenched his hands into fists and counted to twenty-five before she rose up once more. She walked to the center of the room and stood with her arms outstretched and her chin pointed upward.

She waited, still as a carving while the magnificent strains of Tchaikovsky flowed around her. Hunter held his breath. Suddenly she exploded into movement.

"That's my Kat." Slowly he unclenched his hands.

The kitchen light went out, and the studio was plunged into darkness. As music poured into the night a fog settled over the land. Feeling like a thief, he stood outside her window, waiting and watching until at last the music stopped. Then he went to his bed and dreamed that he was searching for Kathleen in the fog.

THREE

Martha was on her second cup of coffee when she saw the wild-haired, bearded man walking toward the kitchen door. At first she thought he must be a beggar or a tramp, but when he came closer, she saw that he was clean and his clothes were well-cut and expensive.

Then what in the world was he doing coming to the back door?

She left her coffee on the table and stood in the doorway with her feet planted wide and her arms akimbo. The sight of all that passive aggression ought to be enough to stop anybody in his tracks. But apparently the man wasn't just anybody, for he merely narrowed his eyes at her and kept on coming. When he was even with the steps, he stopped.

"I came to see Kathleen Shaw." Up close,

lines of fatigue spread out from his bloodshot eyes. Was he a drunk, perhaps?

"There's nobody here by that name." At first the lies had bothered her, but the more she came to know Kathleen Shaw, the more she realized she'd do anything for her.

"And you are . . . ?"

"Martha Kimbrough."

"Ms. Kimbrough, I'm Hunter La Farge."

On closer inspection she recognized the black, piercing eyes from the photograph in the locket, and she didn't have a doubt in the world that he saw her reaction to his name. She tried for a quick recovery, but her sharp intake of breath had already given her away.

"What can I do for you, Mr. La Farge?"

"You can tell Kathleen Shaw that I've come to see her."

"I'm sorry, sir. You must be mistaken. There's no one here by that name."

"She's here. I've seen her."

Martha tried another tack.

"Oh, are you talking about that ballerina that was killed in the boat explosion?" Her laugh wouldn't have fooled a billy goat, much less the man who stood in the backyard as solid as a mountain and just as immovable. "I guess there will always be sightings of famous people. A man at the grocery store the other day swore he saw Elvis on the St. Charles streetcar."

He smiled then, and it was a remarkably

gentle smile, considering that he was such a big man.

"I know about Kathleen, Ms. Kimbrough. I saw her under our tree last night, and I stood outside her window while she danced in the dark." That smile again, so poignant, it almost broke her heart. "Won't you please let me come in?"

Martha dashed a tear from her eye with the corner of her apron. Lordy, she'd always been a sucker for romance. She stepped back and opened the door.

"You can come in, Mr. La Farge, but I can't let you see Kathleen."

He had to duck to fit inside the door.

"Where is she?"

"She's sleeping. Lord knows, she ought to be, dancing all hours of the night, pushing herself till she's near the point of collapse." She got an extra cup from the cabinet. "Coffee, Mr. La Farge?"

"Yes, thank you. And call me Hunter."

She poured a cup and set it in front of him, then took a chair opposite.

"The first word she spoke after the accident was *Hunter*. It was a while before I knew it was your name."

"She called for me?"

"Repeatedly. In her sleep mostly, but sometimes even when she was awake, especially at first."

"She called my name. . . ." He spoke almost to himself, transfixed, seeing things no one else could see.

"Yes." Damned if the woman didn't have to wipe her eyes again. She was turning into a soggy old fool.

He shook himself like a great Labrador coming out of the water, then took a drink of his coffee.

"Everyone thought she was dead," he said. "What happened?"

"It was my brother who found her, out in his fishing boat. He brought her to me first because I'm a nurse and he thought I'd know what to do."

"Where was that?"

"A little village near Cape Town . . . Saldanha. At first we didn't know who she was."

"It was in all the papers."

"Saldanha is not exactly a metropolis. Most folks there don't pay attention to anything except the weather."

"Why wasn't she taken to a large city, to a big hospital? Why wasn't the press notified?"

"She needed immediate attention. Saldanha has a clinic and a village doctor. After she became lucid, she begged us not to tell anyone she was alive."

Hunter pushed his cup of coffee aside. Kathleen. Lying in a remote South African village while he searched the globe for her. She'd been so close. How could he not have found her? Why hadn't he been there when she'd called his name?

"Not even me?" he asked.

"Especially not you."

He didn't have to ask why. He remembered the first time he'd ever seen her cry. She was eight years old and she'd been sitting on the back steps of the schoolhouse, hunched over in a dress that was too big and staring at the hole in the bottom of her shoe.

"Why are you crying, Kat?" he'd asked.

"I'm not crying." She sniffed and rubbed her nose with the back of her hand.

"What'cha doing then?"

"I'm trying to make rocks, see? Mama says if you wish hard enough, you can make anything come true, and I thought I'd be like Moses, see? Only I'm not turning rocks to water, I'm turning water to rocks." She sniffled again, then wadded her hand into a fist. "And when I do, I'm gonna throw them all at old Lola Jean Crumpet."

"How come?"

"For calling my mama a stinking washer-woman."

No, he didn't have to ask why.

Silently, Martha poured out his cold coffee and refilled his cup.

"I love Kathleen," he said. "I never stopped loving her."

Martha Kimbrough stared at her coffee as if

she were trying to make up her mind, then with a long sigh she reached over and patted his hand.

"And she never stopped loving you."

"I want to see her, Martha."

"I don't know. . . ."

Silk skirts rustled in the hallway, and the faint fragrance of gardenia wafted into the room. Hunter froze.

"Good morning, Martha."

When Kathleen appeared in the doorway, Hunter's breathing stopped. In the soft light of morning she was exquisitely beautiful, her long hair tumbled over her shoulders exactly as he remembered and the blush of roses still on her fair cheeks.

But there was something else on her cheeks —a bruise. And two on her arms. There was no telling how many were hidden on her legs underneath her skirts.

Battle scars from her fight to reclaim her dancing skills. Kathleen Shaw had never known how to accept defeat.

She came into the room, moving with the fluid grace that had always been her hallmark. Suddenly her hands flew to her locket and her eyes stared straight at Hunter.

"Martha?"

Hunter stood up slowly like a man in a dream. Kathleen traced the engraving on the face of the locket with her index finger.

"I have the strangest feeling that Hunter is in this room with me. I feel the rush of his blood through my body and the beat of his heart against mine." Clutching her locket, she closed her eyes. "It's almost as if I'm sixteen again and waiting for him to carry me off in that little boat we used to borrow when no one was looking."

Hunter tried to control his breathing. They had made love on that little boat, coupled together sleek as seals with river water sloshing over the sides and the herons calling to them from the swamps.

Kathleen opened her eyes, and once more he had the eerie sensation that she was seeing him. Martha motioned frantically for him to leave, but he could no more leave Kathleen than he could stop breathing.

"Do you think it's this place, Martha, or my own impossible longings?" Kathleen's color deepened, and she pushed her hair back from her forehead in the impatient gesture Hunter had seen her use a thousand times. "Oh, don't tell me I'm foolish. I know that."

She came toward the table then, stopping only inches from where he stood.

"It's this place. It's full of ghosts."

She reached to find her chair, and it took all Hunter's willpower to keep from taking her groping hands and lifting them to his lips. When she was seated, Martha squeezed her hand, then wrote something in her palm.

"Bacon and eggs?" Her laugh was merry. "Goodness, no. If I listened to you, I'd be so fat, I'd roll around the dance floor like a baby hippo. I'm going to sit here in the sun. . . . Martha, why don't I feel the sun coming through the window? Is the shade down?"

Martha's hand flew to her mouth, and Hunter realized he was blocking the sun. He stepped out of its path, then watched the beam of light fall over Kathleen. She turned her face to its warmth, and once more she seemed to be looking straight at him.

"That's better." She drew a long sigh. "I wish I could go out in the sun without my hat and veil."

Martha took her palm and wrote emphatically. Kathleen recoiled.

"And have someone see me like this? 'Poor blind, deaf woman,' they'd say. 'Didn't she used to be a ballerina?' " She stood up and stalked toward the kitchen cabinets. "No! I'd rather be dead." She was moving so fast, she misjudged the distance, and the edge of the counter caught her in the abdomen. Without a word, she straightened herself up, then felt in the cabinets until she found a bowl and a box of cereal. She measured her cereal precisely, using her fingers, then reached into the refrigerator for the milk.

"I will *not* enter the world until I can do it on my own terms." When she jerked out the

milk carton, a jar rolled off the shelf and shattered at her feet.

"Stay right where you are, Martha." Kathleen lifted her chin and turned a fierce proud
stare in Martha's general direction. "It's my
mess. I'll clean it up. And don't you dare tell me
I'll cut myself. I won't."

She felt along the wall until she found the
towel rack, then squatting on the floor, she began carefully to mop up the spilled pickles. Sur-
rounding her were the tools of the blind: a
braillewriter on the small desk beneath the window, a collapsible cane, the hat with the veil.

Hunter felt worse than a thief as he watched
her; he felt like a betrayer. She had the same
strong-willed, stiff-necked pride that he did. If
he had been in her situation, he'd have been
equally determined to make a comeback on his
own terms.

They were one and the same. *You are me and
I am you,* she'd said long ago. And it was still
true.

He had no right to stand in her kitchen and
watch her groping around the floor trying not
to cut herself. By trying to impose himself on
her, he was serving his own selfish needs. Not
hers.

Quietly he let himself out, then stood beyond her kitchen door with his heart bursting
and his throat aching. Inside was the woman

he'd lost . . . twice. And he was in danger of losing her again.

Should he leave and give her the time she wanted, or should he stay? If she found out he'd seen her and then left, she'd surely think it was because of her handicaps; but if he stayed, she'd think it was out of pity.

As he often did when he was faced with a problem that seemed to have no answer, Hunter began to run. The rude cottages on a run-down street gave way to antebellum houses set on guarded lawns. Bells on the trolleys clanged and musicians on street corners called to him to stop and enjoy the music as he raced by. In the distance he could hear chimes from the cathedral intermingled with the blues from a lonesome sax.

Sweat poured down his face and wet the back of his shirt. Hunter sucked oxygen into his lungs and kept on running. He didn't stop until he reached the cathedral.

It was cool and gloomy inside, lit by candles flickering on the altar and faint rays of sun that filtered through stained-glass windows. Winded, heartsick, desperate, he clung to the massive carved archway . . . just as he had the day he'd come home to claim Kathleen Shaw.

"Didn't you get my letters?" his mother had asked him the day he'd docked in *Jefferson Parish.*

"I've been in a damned Congo prison for the last two years."

"*Kathleen's marrying Dr. Earl Lennox.*"

"*Kathleen . . . marrying another man? When? Where?*"

"*Today. St. Louis Cathedral.*"

He'd raced through the streets of New Orleans, trying to make it to the church on time; but he was too late. Just as he burst through the door, the minister pronounced them man and wife.

His howl of anguish rose up from his very soul. "*KATHLEEN!*"

She turned around, and her face became as white as her wedding gown. The look in her eyes pierced his heart, and it lay torn and bleeding somewhere in a body he could no longer feel. Wedding guests turned to stare at him. He was bearded, scruffy, his eyes red-rimmed from the long trip across the ocean.

With his feet planted wide and his hands balled into fists, he stood underneath the archway as he and Kathleen stared at each other. He saw her lips move as she silently spoke his name.

I love you. His lips formed the words. She bent toward him like a willow in a strong wind.

Dr. Earl Lennox offered his arm, and organ music shattered the stillness. Slowly Kathleen turned from him and took the arm of her husband.

"*You came too late,*" she said when she was even with Hunter, and then she passed through the doors and out of his life.

The wedding guests hurried out behind them, and he was left clinging to the archway, chanting her name like a drunken sailor.

Agony rose up in him afresh, and he cried out as he had so many years before.

"KATHLEEN!"

Her name ricocheted off the vaulted ceilings and mocked him.

Kathleen . . . Kathleen . . . Kathleen.

Alarmed, an old priest hurried toward him, his robes rustling in the stillness.

"My son, is there anything I can do for you?"

"No, thank you, Father. It's far too late."

"It's never too late. Would you like to talk about it?"

"Confess my sins?" Hunter's laugh was hollow. "There's not enough grace in the world to cleanse my black soul. Besides, I'm used to hell."

With one last look at the altar rail where Kathleen had pledged herself to another man, Hunter turned and walked from the cathedral.

"Come again," the old priest called after him.

But he knew he wouldn't. The only one who could save him was Kathleen, and she could no longer hear him confess his sins.

It was raining hard when he stepped outside the cathedral. Hunter walked home in the downpour, and the first thing he did when he got there was pick up the phone. There were all kinds of hell, and one of the worst was ignorance.

He dialed the number that was emblazoned in his memory, hoping that Kathleen had done the same as he, kept everything about her childhood home exactly as it had been when they were growing up. Martha answered on the sixth ring.

"This is Hunter La Farge—no, please don't hang up. I need to know the name of the clinic in Saldanha and the name of the doctor who treated Kathleen . . . yes, you heard right. Now that I've found her, I'm never going to let her go again."

It took two hours to locate Dr. Heinrich Garth.

"Damage from the explosion was extensive to the retina," he finally said. "Kathleen Shaw will never see again."

Hunter fought against the dreadful truth. For Kathleen, there had to be a miracle.

"Do other experts concur with your diagnosis?"

"Yes. I had them flown in. One in England, one in France, and one in the United States."

"Surely there is something that can be done."

"There is nothing, Mr. La Farge. I urge you not to build false hopes in this woman. Her vision will never return."

Gripping the phone so hard that his knuckles turned white, Hunter contained his agony.

"And her hearing?"

There was no sound, and for a moment Hunter thought the line had gone dead.

"There is a possibility she will regain her hearing."

"She'll hear again?"

"There are no guarantees."

"What can I do to make it happen?"

Again, the long silence. And then a sigh.

"Pray," Dr. Garth said.

Hunter held the phone long after it was dead. And then the man who had always relied only on himself dropped to his knees and prayed to a god he wasn't even sure existed.

"Martha, is it dark yet?"

According to her braille watch it should be, but Kathleen wanted to make certain.

Martha tapped her once on the hand. *Yes.*

"I'm going to the special tree."

She sensed Martha's agitation. Did she disapprove? Perhaps. Martha was not the kind of woman who would cling to old dreams.

She put on her hat and dropped the veil into place. No sense in taking chances. Outside, she stood for a moment feeling the breeze in her hair.

She wondered if the cicadas were singing.

For a moment she thought she heard them. Cocking her head, she listened. But there was only silence.

As she made her way across the yard she wanted to pull off her shoes to feel the cool tickle of grass on her feet, but she was afraid of stepping on a stick or a stone. She had enough injuries without adding more.

When Spanish moss brushed against her face, she parted its lacy curtain and stepped inside. Instantly she froze. There was a brooding presence about the tree . . . and something else, another presence, big and solid, pulling at her like a magnet.

Hunter. She leaned her head against the trunk and closed her eyes, feeling once more his lips on hers, his hands moving over her body, branding her, possessing her. So real was the vision that she almost sank to the ground and spread herself out to receive him.

She put one hand over her locket to ground herself in reality. Hunter was in Africa, and she was deaf and blind. Period. End of dream.

With her other hand, she pushed away from the trunk—and felt the piece of paper in the knothole. Her hands shook as she pulled it out and unfolded it. Inside lay a heart-shaped locket, the engraving a perfect match to the one that hung around her neck.

Breathless, she traced the fleur-de-lis, and as

she did she felt the raised lettering on the paper. Braille.

My darling Kat . . .

"Hunter?"

She felt his hand on hers, the long blunt fingers, the moon-shaped scar in his palm. He tapped once. *Yes.*

"No! It can't be. I won't let you see me like this."

She tried to run, but he caught her shoulders. Cursing the darkness and the silence, she kicked him on the shin.

"Dammit, Kat! Hold still."

She stiffened. Did she hear him or was it merely her imagination, drawing on ancient memories?

"Did you say something?" She cocked her head, listening for an answer, but there was nothing except the dark night filled with smells and silence.

Hunter lifted her hand to his lips. They were warm and insistent against her palm, setting off such a storm of emotional conflict that her whole body trembled.

"I can't bear it if you kiss me, Hunter. Please, don't."

He released her hand, then gently pressed it to the braille letter. She jerked it away.

"No. I don't want to know why you came or what you have to say. All I want you to do is leave."

He pressed her hand to the letter once more. There was no gentleness in him now, and she knew he would not relent. Hunter's will was as strong as hers, perhaps stronger. He would never back down.

Nor would she.

"No!" she said, and made a move to tear the letter. He put out his hand to stop her. His arm was rigid, and she knew his body would be the same way, as unyielding as the massive trunk of the live-oak tree.

"I'll scream if you don't let me go."

He wrote in her palm with bold, angry strokes.

Scream.

Memories threatened her once more. The last time she'd threatened to scream, they'd ended up on the ground together, joined heart, body, and soul.

They'd both thought it would be forever. Inside, Kathleen wept for the lost innocence of her youth.

She felt the heat of Hunter's body and his warm breath against her cheek. He was so close . . . and yet he might as well still have been in Africa.

"Why did you have to find me?" she whispered.

He lifted her veil and cupped her face. His hands were exquisitely tender as he traced her eyebrows, her cheekbones, her lips. She knew he was going to kiss her; she felt it in the way he held his body, the way he touched her skin.

And she knew she was going to let him. Because she had to. Because she would not be able to live if she didn't feel his lips on hers once more.

Suddenly she was in his arms, pressed hard against his chest, her lips open and waiting for his. The first touch sent shock waves through her. Thirteen long years had dimmed the memories. Reality far exceeded the dreams.

She clung to him, unaware of his groans and her own deep-throated sounds of satisfaction. There was no gentleness in them, but the sharp, all-consuming sensations of being reborn. Taste and feel and smell were heightened until their very skin hummed with the electricity of their kiss.

Pressed tightly against him, she felt her blood leave her body and flow through his, felt the strength of his heart beating in her chest. For a heady moment power and beauty and grace surged through her, so that she believed her life lay just ahead of her, in this city with this man. As his tongue delved into her mouth she was sixteen again and filled with promise.

She wove her hands into his hair. It was longer than she remembered. Was it still as dark as the boot blacking used by the old shoe-shine man on the corner of Bourbon and Canal? It felt as untamed. With his beard he must be an awe-

some sight, every inch the swashbuckling vagabond pirate of her memories. Her Prince
Valiant. Her best friend. Her hero.

As she clung to him she felt all her resolve
crumbling. His body heat melted her, and her
knees started to buckle. Hunter pressed her
against the trunk of the tree, just as he had so
many years ago, and his hands roamed freely
over her body.

He used to murmur her name, over and
over, in a voice so rich and deep with love, it
sounded like music. Was he calling her name
now?

Hunter braced his arms on either side of her
body, and with her back against the tree she felt
the full impact of his passion. He had always
been a turbulent man, full of thunder and lightning and storm winds, and now he raged
through her with hurricane force. All the years
she'd spent with Earl went tumbling away like
chaff before the gale, and she knew that there
had never been another man for her, would
never be another man except Hunter La Farge.

Reason told her to leave immediately, to run
as far and as fast as she could, but passion had
nothing to do with reason. Her body was twisting in the wind, and she was begging to be rescued.

"Hunter . . . oh, Hunter . . ."

Savage, unrelenting, he ground his mouth
and hips against her, and even through their

clothes she felt the sweet hot friction. She slid her hands inside his shirt and sank her fingernails into his back, screaming into his open mouth as the spasms shook her.

He held her, gentling her with his hands, his lips, his tongue. He licked away the sweat that inched down the side of her neck and into her cleavage. Spasms shook her anew as his tongue dipped beneath her neckline and found her taut nipple. With long, sweeping strokes he soothed and provoked until she was pleading once more, his name on her lips like some ancient litany to a demanding god.

Suckling deeply, he pushed aside her skirt and touched her where other men would not dare, touched her in ways that transported her beyond the silent darkness into a world of color and light and music. She danced to the music, faster and faster until all the colors blurred and the light exploded in one bright moment that burned itself forever on her memory.

He captured her lips once more in a kiss as gentle and as necessary as a spring rain falling upon a pregnant earth. And in one blinding epiphany, Kathleen realized that Hunter had given everything and taken nothing. His actions told her more clearly than words ever could that he loved her still, loved her enough to look beyond her infirmities to the passionate woman within.

Thirteen years of longing could be brought

to an end. Months of living in isolation could vanish. All she had to do was open her arms and welcome him home.

"Please, Hunter." She put her fingertips against his lips, then leaned her head against the tree trunk. "Oh, please . . ."

Raw energy pulsed through her fingers. A sense of adventure and daring clung to him, and when she breathed deeply, she smelled the rich jungles of the Congo and the heady excitement of the diamond mines, caught somehow in the pores of his skin.

How could she shackle all that energy? How could she tame all that wildness?

Chaining him to her side would be more than selfish; it would be criminal. Like all fine animals, Hunter La Farge belonged free.

"I don't know what you want of me, Hunter, but whatever it is, it's more than I'm willing to give." She bent to pick up her hat, which had fallen to the ground in their mindless pursuit of each other. "Please leave."

He knelt beside her and tapped her hand twice, vigorously. *No.* Then she felt the braille letter being shoved into her hand once more.

Sighing, she took the letter and sat at the base of the tree. She owed him that much, at least.

❖━━━━━━❖

My darling Kat [it said]. *I know what you're going to tell me. Leave. I can no more leave you than I can stop the sun from rising. I love you, Kat. I've never stopped loving you . . . even the day I stood at the back of the cathedral and watched you marry another man. You were lost to me twice, my darling. I'm never going to lose you again. Whatever you say, whatever you do will not drive me away. I know you, Kat. You're proud and independent and stubborn . . . all the things I love about you. You'll try very hard to send me away, but I will not go. You are my soul. You always have been and always will be. I may never feel you beneath me again, lying under the oak tree with the sun making lacy patterns on your skin. I may never win you back . . . but I'll spend the rest of my life trying.*

She bought time by carefully folding the letter. Then she tucked it into her skirt pocket. Later she'd put it away in a special place, just as she once had put away the letters that had been blown away in the explosion.

"Then you will have wasted your life, Hunter, and you'll have nothing to show for it except gray hair and wrinkles."

Did he laugh? The change in his body language felt like laughter, and it would be typical of Hunter. Laughing at the gods, thumbing his nose at fate.

Suddenly she felt his lips on hers once more,

insistent, persuasive. She fought to hold on to reason, but it went tumbling away in the winds of passion that swept through her. Her only defense was to swat his face away and hide under her hat. As she lowered the veil she felt like a coward.

Hunter grabbed her palm and wrote. *Afraid?*

"Never. Not of you. Not of anyone or anything. I just simply don't have the time to waste with you. I have much more important things to do."

Dance? he wrote.

"How did you know?"

I watched.

"If Martha catches you, she'll call the police . . . and I'll let her." She knew, of course, that her threat wouldn't scare Hunter off. She was merely buying time until she could leave the tree.

Coward, he wrote.

It was her turn to laugh. He was gambling that she'd let him stick around in order to prove him wrong.

"You always were clever, Hunter. It won't work this time. The only person I have to prove anything to is myself."

When she stood up, Hunter caught her hand. It was warm and steadfast, a hand she'd held on to since she was five years old. How could she bear to let go?

As they stood together under the tree the

way they had so many years before, she felt the tremor that ran through him. Hunter was a man of intense feelings, and they'd always shown in his eyes. A great sadness descended on her.

She would never see Hunter's eyes again. In the end, it was that thought that gave her courage. Quietly, she released his hand.

"Eventually you'd feel sorry for me, Hunter. I couldn't bear your pity."

She walked away, counting her steps, and the silent darkness closed around her. Somewhere under the tree, she imagined Hunter watching and waiting.

And that's the way she would always remember him, waiting for her under the live-oak tree with the Spanish moss swaying in breezes from the river and gardenias filling the sultry air with their heady perfume.

FOUR

He knew she wouldn't come to the tree again. As soon as she got back to her house, she'd probably instruct Martha not to let him in the door.

As if that would stop him.

When she was safely inside, Hunter climbed into his car and drove to Loyola. Dr. Brent Myers was still in his office, bent over his braille-writer.

"Hello," he said, removing his thick glasses and rubbing his eyes. "I didn't expect to see you again so soon. Did she get the letter?"

"Yes. I delivered it in person."

"May I be so bold as to ask what her response was?"

Hunter had no qualms about answering such a personal question. He had liked the man on sight. When he'd gone to the university earlier seeking help, Myers had been perfectly blunt.

"I will help you only if you're sincere about this woman," he'd said. "I have no intention of being a party to a cruel hoax."

It hadn't taken long for Hunter to convince Myers of his sincerity. Nor for Myers to win Hunter's respect. Legally blind, Myers still taught nineteenth-century literature to the sighted as well as working in his spare time with the blind.

Now, straddling a chair, watching the professor polish his glasses before returning them to his nose, Hunter answered the question. "Her response was exactly what I expected; she told me to leave."

"A proud woman."

"Yes. And a fighter. One day Kathleen will again be the world's greatest ballerina, and I will be at her side." Intense, Hunter leaned toward the older man. "Can you teach me to read braille?"

"Yes. When do you want to start?"

"Now."

"You have the first criterion of a good student, an eagerness to learn." He motioned for Hunter to move his chair close to the desk. "And so . . . let us begin."

Martha had become a totally shameless woman—accepting bribes.

"I really shouldn't take these," she said, knowing perfectly well she would. How Hunter La Farge had found out she loved Godiva chocolates better than anything else in the world was beyond her. And roses! He'd brought enough roses to fill her bedroom and half the kitchen. "You're the very devil himself."

"At your service."

With a wicked grin that confirmed her diagnosis, he bent over her hand and bestowed a kiss that warmed the cockles of her old heart. Lordy, she was bewitched, and her sixty-eight years old.

"She'll kill me when she finds out," Martha said, knowing Kathleen would do no such thing. Her temper would definitely get in a stir, but she was too much a lady to resort to violence.

Music poured from Kathleen's studio. They could hear the slap of her ballet slippers against the wooden floor and an occasional crash followed by an expletive.

"She needs me," Hunter said, as if he'd read Martha's mind. "When we were children, I'd sit for hours and watch her dance. She used to say I was her courage."

Martha had always prided herself on being a good judge of character, and she'd be willing to stake her life on Hunter's sincerity . . . and his determination.

"I figure you're going to see her whether I

give permission or not." The look in his eyes told her she'd spoken the truth. "We could use some more milk, and the bathroom supplies are getting low."

"Good. It's settled. I'll stay with Kathleen while you're shopping. And Martha . . . take your time. She'll be in good hands."

Martha buried her face in her roses, then smiled at him. "I never doubted that for a minute."

Sweat soaked the front and back of Kathleen's leotard and inched from under her heavy hair. She reached for a towel on the barre to wipe her face. With her hand in midair, she froze.

The haunting sounds of the adagio from *Sleeping Beauty* filled the room. Or was it her imagination? The towel fell from her hand, and she pressed her hands over her ears, afraid to trust the miracle.

To hear music again . . . to move in time to the beautiful rhythms . . . to soar through the air on wings of melody . . . It was a dream beyond imagining.

"Please, God," she whispered. Then slowly, ever so slowly, she took her hands away.

The sounds were there, just as she had imagined, not faint and faraway, but as clear as the chimes that echoed through Jackson Square.

"Martha," she yelled. "Martha!"

She heard the sound of hurrying footsteps in the hallway. Oh, blessed sound.

"I can hear . . . I can hear!"

"Then I want these to be the first words you hear. I love you, Kathleen."

All the months she'd waited in silence for the return of her hearing, she'd dreamed of what she wanted most to hear. And always, it had been the sound of Hunter's voice. Even before the music.

Mesmerized, she stood absolutely still while sound washed over her—the majestic melodies of Tchaikovsky, the tick of the hall clock, the song of a mockingbird outside her window, the scratch of a tree branch along the side of the house, the distant barking of a dog. And Hunter's voice.

"Did you hear me, Kat? I love you. I never stopped loving you and I never will."

"I heard you, Hunter. And it doesn't change a thing."

She could imagine the way he walked by the sound of his boots on the wooden floor, emphatic, measured sounds of a man with a purpose. Suddenly he was beside her, his body heat mingling with hers, his hands upon her face.

"It changes everything," he said, tracing the path of moisture from her cheekbones to the corner of her lips.

She hadn't been aware of tears, only of being drunk with sound.

"No," she whispered.

"Yes." He circled her lips with his index finger. "Now I can say all the things to you that I couldn't put in a letter."

"You've said everything you need to say."

"Except I'm sorry. I'm sorry I ever left you in the first place, sorry the letters stopped, sorry I came home too late." With one hand on her cheek and the other around her waist, he drew her close. "But most of all I'm sorry for letting the music stop for you, Kathleen. I made a sacred vow to you, and I broke it. Can you ever forgive me?"

His voice could persuade saints to turn in their crowns. She imagined how it would be to let herself be persuaded. No more bruising herself against the walls, no more dark lonely hours, no more being one against the world. Just the blessed peace of hiding in the shelter of his love and letting Hunter fight her battles.

"I forgave you a long time ago, Hunter." She hoped he didn't see how dangerously close she was to being persuaded. "For a while I hated you for coming back too late, but Earl was a wonderful man and a good husband. There was no room for hate in my life."

"Did you love him, Kathleen?"

"I married him. That's all that matters."

"Did you *love* him?"

"What do you want me to say, Hunter? That I never loved another man but you? That I never made love to my husband without wishing he was you?" She drew apart from him. "Yes, I loved Earl Lennox."

It was no lie. She *had* loved him as much as she could ever love another man.

"I'm sorry, Kat. I had no right to ask that question. Earl Lennox deserved your loyalty."

"How do you know?"

"I kept up."

"You had me *watched?*"

"Yes. For a while. Until I was certain he would be good to you. And I make no apologies."

"I'd forgotten that about you, Hunter. That you like to be king of the world."

"That's one of the things you loved about me."

She wiped her face with the towel, remembering. He'd been like the young lion they used to visit in Audubon, sleek, beautiful, powerful, sure of his superior position. How she had loved his boldness. And how she loved it still.

But Hunter must never know.

"*Loved* is the operative word."

"Your eyes give you away when you lie. . . . So does your body."

Silently she cursed her own folly. Her leotard would hide nothing, neither the taut ripening of her breasts nor the heavy flutter of her pulse. Casually she flung the towel over her shoulder, then threw back her head and laughed.

"Dancing always excites me, Hunter. I suppose that's one of the many things you've forgotten."

"I've forgotten nothing. Nor have you, Kathleen."

"Dancing is better than sex, Hunter," she teased. She was onstage at the high school, rehearsing for the ballet sequence in Oklahoma! *long after all the other cast members had gone home.*

"Better than sex?" A fierce light gleamed in the center of his eyes as he stalked her.

"Yes." Her laughter was breathless, and already her blood was humming with anticipation. "See what it does to me." She cupped her breasts, lifting them until they almost spilled over the plunging neckline.

"Beautiful lying vixen."

He was standing in front of her now, his feet widespread, his thighs touching hers. Her breath sawed through her lungs.

She caught his dark head as he bent over her. His mouth closed over her nipple, leotard and all. The friction of the wet fabric against her skin sent her spiraling upward until she was almost screaming her pleasure.

Suddenly his mouth left her breasts, and he was laughing down at her.

"Shall we dance, Kat?"

"*Where is the music?*"

He touched his heart, and then hers. "There," he said.

She shoved her leotard aside and wrapped herself around him.

"*Let's dance, Hunter.*"

Joined, they'd waltzed around the stage until the music became a frantic jazz rhythm that sent them to the floor. Afterward Hunter lifted himself on his elbows.

"*Better than sex, Kat?*"

She kissed his lips. "I lied."

"*Lie to me again. I want to prove you wrong.*"

"No, Hunter, I haven't forgotten. We were magnificent together. But all that's in the past."

"And in the future. We will be magnificent together again."

"I'm no longer sixteen. I don't believe in that particular fairy tale anymore."

He didn't answer, but stood for a while searing her with his overwhelming presence. Then she heard him prowling the room. Hunter could never be still when he was disturbed.

"Please leave," she said, even while a part of her mind begged him to stay.

"Not yet, Kathleen."

His measured steps reverberated through her. The path of warmth she'd been standing in vanished, and she knew he was at the window, blocking the sun. Backlit by the sun, he used to look like a god descended from Mount Olympus.

Suddenly darkness overwhelmed her, and she had to bite down on her lips to keep them from trembling. How easy it would be to let herself depend on Hunter.

She felt the sun on her face once more, and the solid disturbing presence of Hunter.

"How long will it take you to make a comeback, Kat?"

"I don't know."

"Make a guess."

"Now that I can hear, perhaps no longer than six months."

"I'll make a bargain with you."

"I've already made my bargain—with myself."

"You were never a coward, Kat."

"No. And I don't intend to be. Don't you see, Hunter? You're so easy to depend upon. If you stay, I'm in danger of becoming a sniveling coward." She held out her hands, and he took them. "Please . . . if you have any regard for me at all, give me the dignity of doing this on my own."

"Can there not be dignity if you have the help of a friend? We were best friends, Kat, long before we ever became lovers."

"Yes, Hunter. We were best friends." He squeezed her hands, nothing more, just the good solid comfort of a friend.

"Let me be your best friend again, Kat, for six months. If at the end of that time you want me to leave, I'll go."

She was tempted, so very tempted. Hunter had taught her to swim and to ride a bike. He'd taught her to swing like a boy with her fists and to bait a fishhook without being squeamish. They'd skipped rocks on the river and sneaked their first smoke together behind the school cafeteria. Once he'd smuggled her into the boys' locker room at the gym because she'd told him she wanted to see if she was getting the best bargain of the bunch.

"I have Martha, who should never have let you in. How did you get past her?"

"I insisted." He turned her hand over and traced a heart in her palm. "Will Martha take you skinny-dipping in the river and motorcycling around the lake? Will she take you flying after dark so you can touch the moon?"

"Don't tempt me, Hunter." She released his hands and stepped back, aware of the burning imprint of the heart.

"Do I tempt you, Kat?"

More than you'll ever know.

It was her turn to prowl the room. Was she strong enough to send him out of her life? Could she survive the pain of losing him once more?

Perhaps not. Perhaps something vital in her would die if she knew for certain that he would never be a part of her life again. Always, always, she'd held on to the dreams, even while she was lying in the hospital bed begging Martha not to let Hunter know she was alive.

She braced herself against the barre, gripping it with both hands behind her back.

"You broke your word once, Hunter. Even then, I waited for you. Two years without a word, not a single letter."

"I spent those two years in a Congo jail."

"Why?"

"For being in the wrong place at the wrong time."

"How do I know you won't be in the wrong place at the wrong time again?"

"The dream I was chasing is dead, Kathleen."

"Your father is dead?"

"I don't know. I never found him. All I know is that it's not important anymore. I am Hunter La Farge."

The long silence screamed through her. Hunter made no move to come close. She remembered how he used to look while he waited, darkly handsome, brooding, filled with subterranean currents she could only imagine. He'd had his say. He would not try to persuade her, either by touch or further conversation.

The choice was hers. Slowly she released the barre, certain of what she had to do.

"I'll give you six months. Just friends."

"Just friends. Unless you ask for more."

"I won't ask."

"I intend to do everything in my power to see that you do."

"You always were a gambling man, Hunter."

"You're more than worth the gamble."

Dangerous currents flowed between them, currents that threatened to sweep her off her feet and suck her under. The gamble she was taking was enormous, bigger even than her gamble to return to the stage. Her blood sang with challenge. She tipped her chin up, her eyes blazing.

"I won't let you move in. Martha is staying."

His chuckle sent shivers through her. How full of self-confidence he was. How full of life. How tempting.

"I like Martha," he said. "We'll teach her to smoke a big cigar and ride a Harley-Davidson."

One of the things she'd always loved about Hunter was his ability to make her laugh. The laughter bubbled up inside her and spilled over, a merry peal that soon had her holding her sides and gasping for breath.

"We might even take her skinny-dipping," he added.

She held up her hands. "Stop before I collapse."

"I used to dream about your laughter, Kat. It's good to hear it again."

"It's good to laugh again. But it's not getting the work done."

The Tchaikovsky ballet had ended and the room was silent.

"I'll put on another song for you. Which one do you want?"

"No. I'll do it. I'm blind, not helpless." She walked to the tape player, counting her steps. "If you're going to be my best friend, the first thing you have to do is to let me be independent."

There was silence. When Hunter finally spoke, his voice was filled with a steely determination.

"Not only will I let you be independent, I will set you free."

"How?"

"If you're going to be my best friend, you have to learn to trust me again." He walked to her and tipped her chin up with one finger. "Trust me, Kat."

It took all her willpower to keep from twisting her hands into his hair and pulling him close.

"I'll try, Hunter."

Trusting him was the least of her worries. It was herself she didn't trust.

FIVE

Kathleen was on her second cup of coffee when the kitchen door opened. She knew it was Hunter even before Martha spoke. The electricity of his presence sent shock waves through her.

"Lordy, Hunter, I didn't expect to see you so bright and early in the morning," Martha said. "But you're always a welcome sight. Do you want coffee?"

"No. I want Kat." Kathleen stood up, her skin humming with excitement. "I have something to give her."

His measured, relentless steps made her think of a stalking panther. When he was close, he reached for her hand. "Come with me."

"Not like that." She removed her hand and put it in the crook of his elbow. "Like this. That way I feel whether you are stepping up or down, turning right or left. You become my guide dog."

"Should I bark?"

"Only if you want to."

Breathless, filled with laughter, she waited. Tension zinged through him and made her fingers tingle.

"When the right moment comes, perhaps I'll howl."

He had once, standing up in their small boat in the bayou, his beautiful body naked and slick with her sweat. Involuntarily she squeezed his arm.

"Ready?" A deep, rich undertone of passion vibrated in his voice.

"Where are we going?"

"You have to learn trust, Kat. This is your first test. Are you coming?"

Intrigued, alive as she hadn't been in years, she'd be a fool to say no.

"Yes."

The screen door popped shut behind her. He shortened his stride because of her, but not enough to make her feel as if she were holding him back.

They were on the worn path between their houses. That much she knew. The smells were familiar, and the beaten smoothness of the ground.

"I should be dancing."

"You're pushing yourself too hard, Kat. You need a break."

What he said was true. The day before, after they'd made their pact, she'd pushed especially hard, perhaps in an attempt to show him that she could make a comeback on her own, that she didn't need help from him or anybody else.

He hadn't tried to stop her. Instead he'd watched from the sidelines, calling his encouragement the way he used to when they were young.

Suddenly she felt herself being lifted off her feet.

"Hang on to your hat," he said.

"Put me down."

"Do you want to fall through the back steps and break your leg?"

"No."

"Then allow me to help you across."

Being in his arms felt wonderful. She had a weak, self-indulgent moment of hoping he'd make some lame excuse to keep holding her. She was even trying to think up a gracious way to accept without losing face when she felt herself being set on her feet.

"Here we are," he said. "Home sweet home."

She smelled the old wax on the linoleum and heard the distinctive tick of the cuckoo clock Janice Smith aka La Farge had kept on the kitchen wall.

"You haven't changed anything," she said, adjusting her veil.

"No."

He didn't have to explain further. She was his soul and he was hers. Neither of them dared change a shrine. The ramshackle cottages where they'd grown up together were almost sacred.

"You won't need your hat in here, Kat. I've closed all the blinds."

She reached for her hat, but his hands stopped her.

"Let me," he said. He removed the hat, then cupped her face and slid his fingers through her hair. "At night I dream about the way your hair used to fall like a curtain around our faces when you were on top."

She didn't trust herself to speak, for she'd be making her own confessions, telling of how he came to her in dreams, and of how she awakened with desire hammering at her until she had to cram the pillow in her mouth to drown out her screams.

His animal heat swept through her like a brushfire as he leaned down and kissed her hair.

"Soon, Kathleen, soon, my love, your hair will curtain us once more." Abruptly he released her. "Now, I have something to show you. Come."

He placed her hand in the crook of his elbow and led her down the familiar hallway to his bedroom. It was filled with his scent, the spicy soap he used, the minty toothpaste, and the heady mix of air and sun and earth that belonged exclusively to Hunter. Even without the smells, she'd have known. How many nights had they lain tangled in his bed while Janice worked the night shift at the factory? How many lazy afternoons had they spent romping in the sunshine while Janice and Karen took their Sunday stroll down St. Charles?

She heard Hunter rambling around in his closet, shoving coat hangers aside and rattling boxes.

"What are you doing?"

"Getting your clothes."

"I'm wearing clothes."

"They won't do. What would people say if they saw my kid brother wearing a dress?"

The simplicity of his plan struck her as brilliant. Hunter was going to pass her off as a boy: that would be her freedom.

"I don't know why I didn't think of that myself," she said.

"You were concentrating all your energies on dancing." He handed her the clothes, a pair of pants with a button-front fly, a big shirt, athletic socks, sneakers, and a soft cap like those worn by newsboys in the twenties.

"Do you think it will work?"

"All I can say is it's a damned good thing you've got ballerina breasts."

"Are you saying I'm flat-chested?"

"It's been a long time since I had the privilege of knowing. Why don't I check them out?"

There was laughter in his voice, and more, ever so much more. She sought to hold on to her resolve.

"Why don't you get out of here and let me dress?"

"I was hoping you needed some help."

"Hunter . . ."

"All right. I'm going." She heard him pause in the doorway. "Pick a name."

"What?"

"We can't be Shaw and La Farge. Pick something else."

"Who is to know?"

"Do you want me to pick one? How about Arbuthnot?"

"How about Bearinski?" How easily they entered the old games.

"Or Cranksnow?"

"Dragonitzin?"

"I prefer Frankenstump."

She fell back against the bed, laughing so hard that tears streamed down her face and she had to hold her sides.

"Oh, Hunter," she said, gasping.

Suddenly he was there, kneeling beside her, tenderly cupping her face.

"It will be you and me, Kat," he whispered, "two against the world. Just the way it used to be."

She closed her eyes, seeing him better that way, picturing how he would look with the sun sliding in from the cracks in the blinds, streaming across his dark hair and touching his black eyes. Like some fine sleek animal, all taut sinew and rippling muscle and raw power. She breathed in his scent, slowly, as she would inhale the aroma of a forbidden dessert. A sudden melting sensation made her body go slack, and she felt his hands tighten on her cheeks.

Unable to prevent herself, she reached for his face and pulled it fiercely toward her. His tongue slid into her hot mouth, gathering her essence as a beekeeper might harvest honey. Her blood hummed along her veins like a river of fire, and she was totally helpless against the onslaught of passion . . . helpless and exultant. The blindness had stripped her of light and color. It had taken away great paintings and glorious sunsets and flower petals floating across placid waters on spring breezes. But it had not taken magnificent hunger and the delicious sense of flying.

"Yes," she whispered, "yes."

Still kneeling, his mouth never leaving hers, Hunter spread her legs and slid between them, crushing her against his body so that she felt melded to him. His tongue plied relentlessly, its assault fierce and tender and so highly erotic that it was not a prelude to love, but love itself, melting her bones and taking away her will.

His mouth left hers, and he licked the side of her throat, murmuring her name over and over, like music, just as she had remembered.

She caught his hair and wrapped her legs around his body.

"Don't stop," she whispered. "If you stop now, I'll die."

"I won't stop until you tell me to." He unfastened her blouse and slid it from her shoulders, then lifted her breasts from their lacy nests and cupped them like two creamy doves.

His mouth closed over her, and she was flung backward and forward at the same time, caught up in sensations from years gone by and sensations entirely new. She felt as if she'd been caught in a swiftly moving current that stripped her of everything except clawing emotion and screaming need.

She arched her back to give him better access, then floated on the currents, reborn.

"I don't plan to tell you *stop* for a very long time."

He drew her deeply into his mouth, not in the gentle manner of Earl Lennox but with the magnificent hunger of a rampaging lion devouring his first kill in days. Hot coals tore loose in her belly and spewed fire throughout her body, so that she writhed in the heat.

Reason told her to stop while she could, but she wanted nothing to do with reason, no part

of discipline and denial. She was in the middle
of a holocaust and only Hunter could save her.

"You will leave me," she whispered as he
made long, sweeping forays with his tongue
down the length of her torso.

"Never."

He shoved her skirt up and pushed aside the
tiny triangle of silk that covered her. She could
feel the heat of his breath against her naked
thighs.

"It doesn't matter anymore. I need you,
Hunter. Ravage me."

The first thrust of his tongue was high and
hard, jerking her upward like a puppet on a
string. He held her there for a screaming eter-
nity, plying his deep magic, while she gripped
the edges of the mattress and held on. Then he
lifted her onto the bed and braced himself over
her, his elbows pinning her arms to her sides.

"This is more than need, Kathleen. It's love.
I love you."

"Don't make me say I love you, Hunter.
Don't make me beg."

"I would never force you to beg for something that's yours, that has always been yours."

She didn't need to see the truth in his eyes;
she heard it in his voice. Selfishly she shoved the
truth aside. It took all her energy to deal with
dancing in the dark; she had none to spare for
Hunter.

"Take me, Hunter. *Now*. Before I die of wanting you."

He understood what she was asking for, not the tenderness of love but the rage of eroticism that would obliterate everything except the hot invasion of swollen flesh and the brimstone that coiled and writhed in her belly. His zipper whispered in the never-ending darkness and the first velvety touch of him wrung a cry from her. It echoed around the still room like the mating call of some wild animal.

"This is not about need, Kat. It's about love."

And then he was in her, wringing the cry from her once more. There was something almost bestial about the way he took her, something raw and primitive that answered the pleas wrenched from her very soul. But underlying it all was tenderness, shining through as plainly as if he'd lit a beacon next to her heart.

"Don't make me love you," she whispered. "Don't."

"You will love me, Kat." His zipper raked against her skin as he slid deeper into her, so deep, he cracked the wall that sealed her heart. "But for now, this is enough."

She arched upward to meet him, trapping him in the cradle of her thighs and rocking with a dizzying rhythm that felt like flying. Holding her tightly around the waist, he flipped onto his back. Her skirt tangled around her midriff, and impatiently she twisted it into a loose knot.

She reached for Hunter's shirt buttons, then leaning over, she stroked his chest with her tongue the way she would the pelt of some fine sleek jungle cat. Her long hair tumbled downward, hiding them in its dark curtain.

He kissed her curtain of hair, laughing softly.

"How did you know, Hunter? How did you know it would be so soon?"

"Because I know you, my love. You're the same as you were when you were sixteen, unbridled and untamed."

"But not as naive." She curled her hands into the fine hair sprinkling his chest and pulled so hard, she wrenched a groan from him. "The old demons still drive you, just as new ones drive me. We'll have our time together, Hunter, nothing held back, nothing denied. Then you will go your way and I will go mine."

Her hips began a slow, seductive dance that brought him off the bed.

"Never." He gripped her waist. "I will never leave you again."

But she knew he would. The restlessness thrummed through him with the force of voodoo drums, and his skin carried the scent of far-off, secret places, of deep rivers and raging waterfalls and jungles rich with diamonds and ripe with decay.

The cadence of the drums beat through Kathleen, and she threw back her head and rode to their rhythms, rode until the drumbeats stilled and there was nothing except the velvet heat of flesh against flesh and the sweet, slow death of love.

Even as she sought to hold the driving secret forces at bay, she realized that Hunter had once more handed her the reins, given her the choices. With a subtlety born of instinct and genius, he'd passed the control to her. Heady with power, lost in passion, she carried them to the edge, so that their cries of release rose up simultaneously like two exotic birds taking flight.

She fell across his chest, hiding both their faces under her long hair.

"I didn't have to muffle my cries in the pillow," she said.

He caught her face between his hands and licked the sweat from her upper lip.

"You've dreamed of me?" he asked.

"Yes."

"Tell me your dreams. I want to make them all come true."

"Today?"

"This very minute. All of them."

"My dreams are more sophisticated now than they were when I was sixteen."

"I'm up for the challenge."

He didn't need words to tell her that. She

could already feel him growing big inside her once more. She'd always marveled at his capacity for love, and it delighted her to know that in that area at least, he had not changed.

"Have you had many lovers, Hunter?"

"They were poor substitutes for you."

"Who were they?"

"It doesn't matter. Nothing matters except you."

"I'm jealous of them all."

"I have ways of driving the jealousy from your mind."

She held her hair back from their faces and arched her back, driving herself closer to the heat, offering herself like a willing sacrificial goddess in some timeless love ritual.

"Drive it from my mind, Hunter," she whispered.

He rolled her onto her back, then stripped off her clothes, slowly, as if he were unwrapping a package he'd waited years to receive. Flushed and languid, she spread herself upon the bed, twisting her body at impossible angles to accommodate his questing tongue.

"I've always remembered the taste of you. Like clover." His voice was thick, drugged, as he tore aside his own clothes. "I can never get enough of you."

Spasms rolled over her like waves from the sea as he delved deep into her once more. Like the sweet red clover blossoms, she gave up her nectar and he sucked it with magnificent greed.

"I shall die of this pleasure," she whispered.

"Not yet, my love. Not yet."

He surged over her, oceanlike, covering her with breakers that tore her loose from her moorings and set her adrift. She caught him to her breast, content to drift through the sunlit morning and into the lazy afternoon, never giving thought to time or place. For her there was only the reality of Hunter and the explosive journey of the senses they'd embarked upon.

She lay curved against him, the sun through the blinds making patterns on her skin. Exhausted and flushed from an excess of love, she slept.

Hunter lifted her hair and kissed the nape of her neck, careful not to wake her.

You will leave me, she'd said.

Somewhere deep in the Congo was a faceless, nameless man who was his father. Hunter felt the old familiar tugging inside, heard the siren song beckoning him. He'd been so close, so many times. But each new lead had proved to be a wild-goose chase, a dead end.

The man who had given him life would never give him a name. Hunter would never know who he was, only that he bore a fictitious name his mother had found in a novel.

"Hunter?" Kathleen awakened slowly, her beautiful eyes focused on a point just beyond his face. Slowly she reached out and touched his cheek. "Thank you."

He caught her hand to his face and held it there. "This is only the beginning for us, Kat."

"Let's not talk about the future." She stretched with the languid grace of a cat, totally unselfconscious in her nakedness. "Let's get dressed and prowl around the French Quarter in the sunshine. It is still shining, isn't it?"

"Yes."

"Good. We'll be Jack and Eddie Archibald." She grinned wickedly at him. "Just brothers."

"Which one are you?"

"I'm Jack. Remember Carl Sandburg's Jack?"

They used to sit under their tree and take turns reading poetry to each other. Sandburg had been one of their favorites.

"I remember everything I ever did with you."

Even in repose she had a ballerina's grace. He traced the line of her body from breast to hip, delighted with the shivers that ran through her.

"Hunter, please." She held his hands against her breasts for a moment, then forcefully pushed them away. "Would you keep me here in this bed all day?"

"Yes."

"Next time, perhaps. But you have to bring food. Right now I'm hungry, and I want to go out into the streets and be a swarthy, swaggering son of a gun . . . and then I want to go down to the river."

She felt the stillness in him. He knew without being told that she wanted to confront one of her demons.

"You're certain?"

"I'm certain."

Hunter left the bed, and she heard him scuffling around on the bedside table. "We'll start with the mustache." The bed creaked once more under his weight. "Allow me."

On her knees in the middle of the bed, she puckered her lips and presented them to Hunter.

"Ready," she said.

His kiss was swift and thorough. Her response was wanton and wild.

"You certainly are," he said. "We could wait until tomorrow to go down to the river. Or next week."

"Hunter!"

"All right." He applied the mustache, spending more time than was absolutely necessary.

"How do I look? Will I pass for a boy?"

She scooted off the covers and paraded around the bed. So sassy and self-confident was she that he'd never have guessed she was blind.

"Not with that body."

"Well, I don't plan to go down to the river naked." With hands on her hips she faced him, full front. "But I make no rash promises about what I'll do once I get there."

Hunter laced his hands behind his head and leaned back on the bed to watch her dress. Safe in the cocoon of his cottage, he felt eighteen again. But somewhere deep inside was the nagging certainty that he could never be eighteen again, that no matter how hard he tried, he could never recapture the youthful dreams, never remold the present into the past.

Kathleen leaned over and twisted her tumbled hair into a knot, then tried to stuff it under her cap. Dark glossy curls escaped around her face. With the mustache, she looked like a beautiful Botticelli painting that someone had tried to desecrate.

"Did I get it all tucked in?"

"Not quite."

He left the bed and carefully tucked all the stray hair inside the cap. Then he leaned down and kissed her lips one last time.

"Hmmm," she said. "You taste good, Eddie."

"Thank you, Jack."

Her laughter buoyed his spirits as he put on his clothes. Perhaps, after all, they could recapture the dreams.

SIX

Her mustache itched. But Kathleen considered it a small price to pay for freedom.

She sat on the St. Charles streetcar listening to the talk swirl around her. Two women on the seat behind her were engaged in a conversation about someone called Louise.

"And I said to her, Louise, if you don't stop that drinkin' and carrin' on, Henry's gonna leave you, then what you gonna do?"

"What did Louise say?"

"Why, she reared back and looked at me with them big ol' blue eyes of hers and said, 'Margaret, Henry ain't never gonna leave me 'cause he's got better sense. Where else would he find a woman that'd put up with his gamblin'?'"

Their voices told her what the speakers looked like, midforties or early fifties, sturdy salt-of-the-earth women with careworn faces and stout hearts.

Hunter leaned close. "Are you okay?"

"Exhilarated. A bit apprehensive. Is anybody suspicious?"

"Nobody's given you a second glance—except that young woman who got on two blocks back. Do you think we should ask her to join us for a beer?"

"Don't you dare."

She didn't expect to be scared, but she was. For months she'd lived in isolation under the watchful eye of Martha. She knew where everything in her house was. Nothing was ever out of its place. If she put down a braille book, she could come back two hours or even two days later and find it in that same place. Until Hunter came back into her life, her routine had been strict. Nothing unexpected happened. Everything around her was familiar and therefore comforting.

Now, as they hurtled through the darkness in a streetcar, the world around her seemed chaotic. If she reached her hand out, she didn't know what she would touch. She couldn't see the people around her. For all she knew, they could be muggers or would-be assassins. She had no idea where she was.

"I'm here," Hunter said, as if he'd read her thoughts.

"I know. I'll be all right in a while. Right

now I'm suffering from sensory overload." She squeezed his arm. "I guess I'm not as brave as I thought."

"You're the bravest person I know, Jack, a swarthy swaggering son of a gun." There was a chuckle in his voice.

"Thanks, Eddie."

They got out at Canal, and she held tightly to his arm while they made their way across the noisy street and into the French Quarter. The sounds and smells were almost overwhelming, the clip-clop of horses' hooves, the wail of a lonesome sax, the staccato of tap-dancing shoes on the sidewalk, vendors calling out their wares, tourists jostling and chattering, the sweet aroma of jasmine mingled with the smell of bourbon and the acrid scent of tobacco smoke.

"We don't have to keep going," Hunter said.

"Yes, I do. I can't hide forever."

That's exactly what she'd been doing, *hiding*. All the months since the explosion she'd told herself she was protecting her identity until she was ready to return to the world on her own terms, but now she realized she'd been afraid.

The sight she'd taken for granted was gone forever. True freedom would not come until she'd learned to adjust to a world she could no longer see.

"Let's eat something and then I want to start all over," she said.

"From what point?"

"From the point where we got on the street-car. And then I want you to describe each street as we pass by, including the number of telephone poles, and tell me precisely how many blocks to Canal."

"You can't learn everything in one day, Kat."

"No, but I can start."

"If you weren't wearing that mustache, I'd kiss you."

"If you could find a deserted alley, I'd let you anyhow."

"Hang on."

Laughing, he hurried down the street, then ducked around a corner. Suddenly she found herself in his arms, his lips on hers.

"I've always wanted to kiss a woman with a mustache."

"Liar."

The kiss was intense and thorough. And it told her more vividly than words that she was not alone.

"Someday you're going to be king of the world," she whispered.

"And very soon you're going to be the world's greatest ballerina."

They had shrimp po'boys at Napoleon House, then retraced their steps, with Hunter giving a running commentary all the way. Kathleen tried to remember every small detail. She couldn't depend on Hunter forever, and she would never be truly free until she could make the journey alone.

She felt her braille watch. Four o'clock.

"Do we have time to go down to the river?" she asked.

"Our special place is waiting there, just for us."

This time they didn't have to steal a boat to get to the bayou. Kathleen was almost sorry. She felt as if she'd stepped back in time. Alone with Hunter on the river, she put aside all her demons and let her mind drift in peace. Even though she could no longer see the sun on the water and watch the Spanish moss sway as their boat passed silently by, she could smell and she could hear. And most of all she could feel.

She felt wonderful, alive, full of possibilities. The boat rocked and swayed, and she lifted her face to the warmth of the sun.

"We're rounding the bend into our private place, Kat. You can take off your hat if you want to. The mustache too. There's no one to see except a pair of wood ducks floating around in the shallows."

How like Hunter to understand that she needed to feel the breeze in her hair. She pulled off the mustache and the cap and immediately felt the lift of the wind.

"Let's pretend, Hunter."

It had been one of their favorite pastimes. *You be king of the world and I'll be your queen,* she'd say. Or sometimes, when she was feeling especially sassy: *I'll be queen of the world and you'll be my slave.*

"What do you want to pretend, Kat."

"That I see desire in your eyes."

"We don't have to pretend that. You do."

They swayed to a halt and water sucked against the paddles as he pulled them into the boat. His hands were hot against her scalp as he wove them into her hair. She tipped her face up so she could feel his warm breath against her lips.

"I want to swim, Hunter."

"You don't have to do this, Kat."

"Yes, I do. I won't let fear win."

Suddenly she trembled, remembering. The heat from the explosion had burned her skin and the waves had closed over her, black and frightening. She'd fought them, thinking it was her tears that made it impossible to see.

Hunter's arms tightened around her.

"I won't let you go, Kat."

"Promise. Promise you won't let me go."

"I promise."

They undressed, then he held her close as they slid into the water. She wrapped her arms and legs around him and buried her face against his neck.

"It's all right, Kat. I'm here. I won't let you go."

"I feel like a coward."

"Let's get back into the boat. There's no need to push yourself like this."

"No. I must do this, Hunter." She sank her fingernails into his upper arms. "I *must.*"

He kissed the droplets of river water from her face, starting with her eyebrows and working his way down to her mouth, all the while holding her in the protective lee of his body.

She took one last bit of courage from his kiss, then drew a deep breath.

"Now, Hunter. Let me go."

"I'll be within arm's reach, Kat."

But what if he weren't? What if something happened, a sudden storm that separated them, or a heart attack or an explosion? She'd be left all alone in the dark water.

Kathleen bit her lower lip to still the panic.

"Now," she whispered, and slowly she felt herself drifting away. She fought the urge to flail her arms and cry out. One stroke, and then two. And she was swimming.

"To your left," Hunter said. "I'm right beside you."

"Don't touch me. I have to do this on my own."

"I won't. Now . . . turn. That's right."

Even in the water, she could feel his reassuring presence. She concentrated all her senses on her task. Up ahead was the boat, a solid object changing the pattern of the waves. With increasing confidence, she swam toward it.

"*Brava*, Kat. *Brava*."

Triumphant, she touched the side of the boat.

"One demon down, many more to go," she said.

He slid through the water and wrapped his arms around her.

"Let's forget about demons for a while, Kat."

They came together with the force of a heat-seeking missile exploding its target. With Hunter buried deep inside her, the water became an ally. He slid against her, sleek and wonderful, and the water swirled around them, bathing them in mystery.

"I could float like this forever," she whispered.

"It will be forever. I promise."

In the darkest corners of her mind, where the truth dwelled, she knew it would not be so. Wanderlust filled him. She could smell it in the air and feel it in the sweet, hot jet he spilled in her.

But she kept her silence. She'd take the moment, and when the time came for him to leave, she'd pick up the pieces of her heart and pretend it wasn't broken.

Hunter eased them into the boat, and she pulled him down to her once more.

"Feel the sun, Hunter? How long before it goes down?"

"About an hour, Kat."

"Let's not waste a minute of it."

The rhythms of an ancient love song overtook them, and the boat began to sway. Kathleen opened her arms and her heart to the melody.

Rick Ransom was waiting for them when they got back home, his red hair gleaming in the feeble light from the naked bulb that hung over Hunter's back door.

A sense of foreboding filled Hunter. Instinctively he put his arm around Kathleen, as if he knew that the news Rick brought would tear them apart.

"Hunter?" She tipped her face up toward his. "What is it?"

"It's Rick Ransom. He's sitting on the backdoor steps."

Except for her hand tightening on his arm, she showed no signs of turmoil. Rick had been her friend too. She knew he could be trusted.

"He doesn't know about me?" she asked.

"No."

"Then I expect he's going to be very surprised."

"This will be a supreme test of your disguise."

Hunter moved forward slowly, reluctant to give up his secret. Over the last two days he'd almost convinced himself that he and Kathleen could stay as they were forever, hiding out in their childhood homes, depending exclusively on each other, and only venturing out into the world when it suited them.

"Rick, what brings you here?" Postponing the inevitable, he angled his body so that Kathleen was partially hidden.

"That's a hell of a question. You leave me hanging on the phone, and I don't hear from you for days. What do you think brought me here?"

"Not any thought of protecting my ornery hide. You know me too well to think I can't take care of myself."

"Yep. I know you too well." Rick fanned himself with his safari hat, then mopped his face with a blue bandanna. Pinching his nose in concentration, he peered through the early-evening gloom, trying to get a better view of Kathleen. "Aren't you going to introduce me to your friend?"

Suddenly Kathleen released Hunter's arm and stepped apart from him.

"Hello, Rick," she said.

He stared at her with genuine puzzlement, then comprehension dawned.

"That voice . . . Kathleen? It can't be."

"Back from the dead," she said.

"By George, this is wonderful. Amazing. No wonder I didn't hear from Hunter."

Fifteen years earlier he would have grabbed his childhood friend into a bear hug, but age and distance had brought restraint. Rick held out his hand. It wavered between them like a lost bird while Kathleen stood facing a point just beyond him and to the right.

"It's really great to see you, Kathleen," he added, reaching forward to clasp her hand.

"It's good to see you, too, Rick."

Hunter made a careful mental note. Kat continued to speak as if she had her sight. Another sign of strength, another sign that she didn't want pity.

"Mosquitoes will be coming out in force soon. Why don't we all go inside for a drink?"

"I could use one," Rick said. "And then maybe you'll explain why Kathleen is wearing a mustache. . . . Not that it doesn't look good on you," he added, turning to her. "You could wear a full beard like Hunter and your beauty would still take my breath away."

Inside, Kathleen stripped off the mustache, then took off the cap and shook out her hair. Desire almost sent Hunter to his knees. While he made the coffee she explained the reason for her disguise to Rick. Hunter watched her with a secret, covetous passion that bordered on obsession.

God, what would he do if she ever turned away from him? How would he survive?

The coffee cups rattled when he set them on

the table. Kat's head came up and her stare miraculously found his face.

She'd always been a delicious witch, divining his thoughts sometimes even before he could get them straight in his mind.

"Well, I guess you're all wondering why I *really* came," Rick said.

Kathleen's fingers turned white around her cup. Hunter reached for her hand and drew it to his lips.

"As you know," Rick continued, for Kathleen's benefit, "Hunter's been looking for his father for many years."

"Yes. I know."

All Hunter's senses went on alert, and he felt the insane urge to smash a fist into Rick's face and toss him out into the yard.

"Well, it seems he's finally turned up."

It doesn't matter anymore, Hunter wanted to shout. But he was powerless. Somewhere deep inside him was a little boy desperately yearning for a scrap of information to prove that the father who had been glamorized to him during his childhood actually did exist.

He's an adventurer, his mother used to say. *A grand and handsome man. I gave him my heart, and when he set sail for Africa, he gave it back to me.* She would touch Hunter's face. *You're my heart. He gave you to me.*

She'd made it all sound mysterious and romantic. His father had lived with the Bushmen in the Kalahari Desert, she said, and with the silverback gorillas in the Congo, scaled the peaks of Kilimanjaro, hunted the wildebeests on the veld, pitched camp in sight of the thousand-foot wall of spray from Victoria Falls, the "smoke that thunders." He was tall and spare, with riveting blue eyes and a star-shaped scar on his cheek. His hair was black as night, and sometimes, when he let it free of the ponytail, it reminded her of the mane of one of the fine racing horses she used to see in her beloved native Kentucky.

His mother told him everything about his father except his name.

They call him Mongo and the Black Knight, and some even call him King. A name doesn't matter, Hunter. It's what you make of it that counts.

Finally he'd stopped asking, but never had he stopped wondering. And now Rick was about to supply the name. In spite of himself, he leaned forward.

"He calls himself Tokolosh."

Tokolosh. From native folklore. A creature of supernatural powers. A chill swept over Hunter's soul.

"That's it?" Hunter asked. "Just Tokolosh?"

"That's it. He was asking about you down in a bar on the Gold Coast."

"Hell, anybody could be asking for me on the Gold Coast. My name is not unknown in Africa."

"Your name is a household word," Rick said. "Sure, anybody could be asking about you, but this man was different. He said, 'I hear Hunter La Farge has been looking for me. Anybody who knows him can tell him I'm finally ready to be found.'"

"Probably some con man looking for a fast buck."

Rick went very still, turning his glance from Hunter to Kathleen then back again. Every nerve ending in Hunter's body screamed.

"He had a star-shaped scar on his cheek," Rick said.

Kathleen's face turned white. She'd heard all the stories too. Hunter left his chair and placed his arm around her shoulders.

"It doesn't matter anymore, Rick."

Kathleen toyed with her coffee cup, saying nothing.

"I can tell you right now that I'm bushed," Rick said, pushing back his chair. "It's a god-awful trip from Johannesburg to Jefferson Parish."

"You can stay here," Hunter said. "I have a spare bedroom."

"Nope. I'm already booked at the Hotel St. Helene. See, the *real* reason I came is to sit in the courtyard sipping mint juleps and watching the long-stemmed Louisiana beauties walk by."

"Call tomorrow after you've rested up,"

Hunter said. "You can bring me up to date on the mines."

Suddenly Kathleen stood up. "You don't have to leave on my account, Rick."

"I'm not."

"Yes, you are," she said. "You've come all the way from Africa. You and Hunter have important things to talk about, and you're rushing off because this whole business is making you uncomfortable."

"Kat . . ." Hunter said.

"I'm not finished yet, Hunter. Let me finish." Her long, heavy hair was still wet from the river. Impatiently she pushed it away from her face. "I want you to stay, Rick. Tell Hunter everything about the man who claims to be his father."

"Kat. Don't."

"You cannot dismiss this, Hunter. Until you know more, you cannot possibly make a rational decision." Her hands moved across the table until she found her cap. "Good night, Rick. It was good to see you again."

"I can't tell you what a thrill it's been, Kathleen, a genuine thrill."

"I'll walk you across." It was not a suggestion, but a command. Hunter backed it up by taking her arm.

"No, thank you, Hunter. I know the way."

A heavy silence fell over the room. Kathleen stood perfectly still in Hunter's grip. She could feel the tension in him. One thing she'd learned over the last few months was patience. Instead of shaking his arm loose, she waited, wondering whether Hunter would pass the test.

Slowly he released her.

"Thank you, Hunter," she said.

"I'll see you in the morning, Kat."

"Yes, Hunter. In the morning."

It took all her willpower to leave. Rick had come from the dark continent, bringing a piece of Hunter's past, and she could feel its siren song echoing through Hunter's blood. Her heart hurt. As soon as she was outside, she pressed her hand over her chest, thinking she might feel it cracked and bleeding.

Moans like those of an animal in pain echoed in the night, and she pressed her fist over her lips. She had no one to blame for the agony she felt except herself. She'd known from the beginning that Hunter wouldn't stay, *couldn't* stay.

And yet, she'd hoped. . . .

As she passed by their tree she heard the whisper of moss in the summer wind, like ghost voices, saying one word over and over. Good-bye. *Good-bye.*

"I made cake for you and Hunter," Martha said when Kathleen reached cottage.

"Hunter won't be coming."

"Well, here, then. You sit and have some. You look a bit tired."

"Thank you, Martha. I think I'll wait a little while on the cake."

"That's a good idea. Don't want to spoil your dinner. Why don't you go and rest while I put it on the table."

"There's something I have to do first."

Martha twisted her hands into her apron as Kathleen passed through the kitchen and down the hall. Soon music poured from the studio, and with it the sound of ballet slippers hitting the wooden floor.

Martha beseeched the ceiling.

"Dear Lord in heaven, what's to become of her?"

SEVEN

"It's amazing," Rick said after Kathleen left. "How did you find her?"

"I didn't find her. Fate brought us back together. And I'll be damned if I'm going to leave her again. *Ever.*"

"My timing and my judgment were both off."

"No. You did what you had to do. Bring me up to date on the mines."

"You don't want to hear about this Tokolosh character first?"

"No. As far as I'm concerned, he's already in hell. He might as well stay there."

Rick poured himself another cup of coffee, then sat back down at the table to begin the long, detailed report on La Farge Diamond Company. By the time he'd finished, they were famished. Hunter ordered pizza, and they ate it with single-minded concentration.

"This man could be the real thing, you know," Rick said, as if he were reading Hunter's mind.

"I know."

"I could have an investigator check him out."

"No." Hunter crammed the pizza scraps into the garbage can and slammed the lid. "Let sleeping dogs lie."

"If you're sure that's what you want."

"I'm positive."

Rick stood up, stretching and yawning. "I'm bushed. I really am going this time."

"How long are you planning to stay?"

"A few days. I thought I'd visit the relatives, maybe call a few old girlfriends and play the big-shot rich guy. Do you think the hat makes me look sexy?"

"The women won't be able to resist you," Hunter said, chuckling.

"Your eyes glow like the pits of hell when you lie."

"How do you know what the pits of hell look like?"

" 'Cause I've been living there for years."

"You hate Africa, don't you?"

"I'm not like you, Hunter. All that untamed land suits you. All that blasting into the earth and wrestling out its treasures." Suddenly self-conscious, Rick crammed his hat onto his head. "Hell, don't pay any attention to me. It's all this moonlight and magnolias that have me crying in my beer."

"Want me to call a cab?"

"No. I've just got my duffel. I'll catch the trolley." He shook Hunter's hand, then squeezed his shoulder. "I'll call you."

As soon as Rick left, Hunter hurried over the path to see Kathleen. Her house was dark and silent.

Kathleen.

Standing in the darkness, he saw a shadow pass across her window.

I love you, Kathleen.

She stood at the window, her white gown glowing in the moonlight.

I won't leave you again.

The shadow moved away. Hunter could hear his blood throbbing through his veins. He threw back his head, and a sound, half moan, half howl, rose up from his chest and echoed through the night.

As he made his way back to his empty cottage, he thought about Kathleen and Rick. When he'd left for Africa, one had stayed behind and one had followed. And he'd failed them both.

"I won't fail you again, Kathleen," he whispered.

He undressed in the dark and lay in his

lonely bed. Just as sleep began to claim him, he thought of the man who called himself Tokolosh. Could he really be telling the truth?

Kathleen sat on the padded bench in front of her dressing table, fully dressed. She opened her watch and ran her hand over its face. Five A.M. And already she'd been up an hour.

She picked up her hairbrush and ran it through her hair. If a hundred strokes were good for it, then two hundred would be better. She heard the tiny sparks of static electricity as she raked the brush through her long silky tresses.

Would Hunter be sleeping? Passion smoked through her, and she had to curl her arms around herself to keep from crying out. No sense in waking Martha. She worried too much as it was.

Kathleen laid down the hairbrush and checked her watch once more. Five-thirty. Would he be up yet?

Unable to sit still any longer, Kathleen got a veiled hat from the closet and quietly let herself out the door. Dew clung to her shoes and wet the hem of her long skirt.

She felt his presence long before she arrived at the tree. A melting sensation overtook her loins, and she had to stop to get herself under control.

How could she send him away if her body kept betraying her?

"Kathleen."

He caught her hand and pulled her through the curtain of moss. His arms were strong around her, and for a moment she leaned her head against his chest, breathing in his scent.

"I couldn't sleep," she said.

"Neither could I."

She felt the tremor that ran through him. Suddenly his mouth was on hers and she was clinging to him, hungry, desperate, unable to let go. His hands moved over her body, and she felt all her defenses crumbling. Soon, very soon, she'd lose herself. She'd lie on the damp grass behind the soft summer curtain of moss pressed so close against Hunter that she couldn't tell where she left off and he began.

"Don't," she whispered. "Oh, please, don't make me need you."

Still holding her close, he dropped her veil back into place.

"You might as well tell me to stop breathing, Kat. As long as I have breath in my body, I'll try to make you need me."

"I don't want to want you, Hunter. I don't want to need you."

"Nothing has changed."

"Everything has changed." She felt the first warm rays as the sun began to climb the sky. "We must go inside. I can't risk detection." He parted the lace curtain, and she held tightly to his elbow. "Hurry, Hunter. Please hurry."

He picked her up and carried her. Underneath the veil she set her jaw in stubborn lines. *Nothing* would make her change her mind, not the way her blood raced or the way his heart pounded against hers, not the melting heat of her loins. She was already a prisoner of darkness; she would not be a prisoner to passion.

Inside the door he tightened his hold on her.

"Put me down, Hunter."

"I should never have stopped at the door."

"You're an honorable man."

"Don't count on it. Do you know what I want to do, Kat?" Her heart slammed against her ribs as she waited for him to speak. "I want to carry you to my bed and bury myself in you so deep that nothing can separate us." He flung aside her hat and buried his face in her hair. "You're my life, Kat. I'll never let you go."

Breathing became difficult. Kathleen clung to the last of her willpower, hoping she had enough to get her through the conversation with Hunter and back to her cottage.

"Let me go, Hunter."

"Only for the moment."

He set her on her feet, and she made her way into his kitchen. A chair that hadn't been pushed back to the table was suddenly in her path, and she was moving too fast to stop. It crashed to the floor.

"Are you all right?" Hunter gathered her into his arms, running his hands down her body. "Did you hurt yourself?"

The rage she'd kept bottled up for months suddenly spilled over.

"No, I'm not all right. I'm blind and it's never going to get any better." She jerked out of his grasp and bent to pick up the chair.

"Kat . . . don't."

"Don't? Don't what? Don't tell the truth? Don't get mad?" She threw the chair as hard as she could and heard it bounce against the wall. "I'm mad, Hunter. I'm damned mad. I want to *see*. I don't want to be dependent on the kindness of strangers to keep from my running into furniture and stumbling over curbs."

"You don't have to depend on the kindness of strangers. You have me."

"I will not be somebody who has to be taken care of."

"Dammit, Kat. This is not about taking care of you. It's about love. I love you."

"You love your vision of me."

There was a thundering silence. She could feel Hunter's anger heating to the boiling point.

"And what do you love, Kat?" His voice was silky and deadly. "Yesterday in my bed when you were screaming my name, what did you love? Some fanciful memory or the flesh-and-blood man you clung to?"

"Damn you, Hunter."

"Damn me all you like, Kathleen. You can't change the truth." He caught her shoulders. "That was *love*, Kat. I'm in your blood the same way that you're in mine, and nothing you can say will ever change that."

His body heat seared her even through their clothes. She could hear the harsh rise and fall of his breathing, could picture the fierce light that shone in his black eyes.

Dear Lord in heaven. He was going to be next to impossible to resist. As desire coiled through her she wondered if she even wanted to resist. How easy it would be walk down the hall and lock the door. How easy to lose herself in the magnificent primeval dance that made all others seem meaningless.

"I will not be persuaded, Hunter. And I will not hang around until this passing fancy of yours turns to pity."

"Is this pity, Kat?" He slammed his mouth down on hers and ravaged her with his tongue. The fires they'd kindled the day before had merely been banked, and his new assault brought them to full flame. Her knees began to buckle, and he caught her with an arm around her waist.

"Or this?" he said as he shoved aside her skirt and roughly dragged her hips into his. Her breath sawed through her lungs as he ground against her.

"You won't succeed with your barbaric tactics."

"Tell me it's pity, Kat. Say that you don't make my blood boil . . . that you don't feel the heat."

"You always were virile, Hunter. That hasn't changed."

Suddenly all the rage went out of him, and he smoothed down her skirt then stroked her cheeks.

"You are my life, Kat," he said. "That hasn't changed. It will never change." He traced her lips, and unable to resist, she licked the tips of his fingers.

Passion swept through her like a firestorm, and she closed her eyes, melting, consumed.

"Six months, Kat," he whispered. "Don't deny us six months."

Six months of delicious eroticism. The sun sliding over her skin as Hunter plowed deep inside her. Her cries of pleasure beating upward like the powerful wings of eagles. The sweet, salty taste of him. Limbs entangled, slick and shining with their combined sweat. His head on her pillow. Never being alone in the dark.

She trembled. Some sacrifices were unbearable.

She covered his hand with hers and with great deliberation sucked his index finger. The passionate rumblings that rose in his throat were like the growl of a great wolf. Every nerve ending in her body screamed for relief.

Kat ignored her traitorous body. She had to be strong. She had to challenge Hunter on equal terms. Weakness would be their undoing.

"Kat . . . you're driving me mad."

He bent down and circled his tongue around her nipple, wetting the front of her blouse. Then he took her deep into his mouth, suckling until she felt the hot, hard tremors of release.

Shaken by the depths of her own passion, she disentangled herself and took a step back.

"I would be a fool to deny the passion between us, Hunter. It has a life of its own." She made her way to the kitchen table, needing to put more distance between them. With her back pressed against the edge of the table, she turned to him. "If we give in to this passion now, it will destroy us both."

"It will save us both."

"No. Already I can think of nothing except being in your arms."

"That's where I want you. Always."

"The man who might be your father is waiting for you in Africa."

"It doesn't matter anymore."

"Yes. It still matters."

Hunter might lie to himself, but he would never lie to her. She heard his footsteps as he went to the sink and drew water. He pressed a tall, cool glass into her hand, then pulled out her chair.

"Nothing is important enough to make me leave you, Kathleen." His chair scrapped against the hardwood floor.

"I won't be your jailer."

"If your arms are a prison, I would willingly die there."

Kathleen couldn't help but smile. Hunter still had poetry in his soul.

"See," he said. "I've made you smile. That's a good start."

"Don't be fooled by my smile. It hides a will of iron."

Hunter's laughter ricocheted off the kitchen walls.

"You've forgotten, my love. I have the blow-torch."

"Damn you."

It wasn't his magnificent arrogance that angered her, but her reaction to it. She felt challenged, revitalized, as if she were a sun-starved philodendron that someone had just put in a window with eastern exposure.

"You *have* to go," she added. "If you don't find out whether this man is your father, you'll always wonder."

"I'm a La Farge. My name is what I've made it, Kat. I don't need the name of some stranger."

"I understand that. But you need to *know*, Hunter."

"I left you once, Kathleen. I will never leave you again."

"Then I have no choice but to leave you."

She pushed back her chair and stood up. Poised for flight, she fully expected Hunter to reach out and grab her wrist or to stand up and block her exit to the door or even to lift her into his arms and carry her off as a lion would his hard-earned quarry. He made no move. The electric silence sent shivers along her skin.

She had almost gained the door when his voice cut through her like a whip.

"You forgot your hat." His boots thundered across the floor, and she felt the hat being shoved into her hand.

With her chin thrust out, she rammed the hat onto her head and lowered her veil. Suddenly she felt suffocated. She balled her hands into fists and took deep breaths.

Hunter opened the door for her. God, he was making it so easy. Too easy.

Bright sunshine poured through the doorway. Only yesterday she and Hunter had lain together in its hot rays in the bottom of a small skiff, their laughter as sharp and clear as the birdcalls from the bayou.

Sometimes yesterdays vanished so quickly.

"You were right, Kathleen." His voice cut

through her reminiscing. "I was in love with a vision."

She stood perfectly still, one hand unconsciously clutching her locket.

"The woman I knew would never run away," he added. "The Kathleen Shaw I loved fought for what she wanted."

She was glad the veil hid her face.

"I'm fighting for what I want. I want to dance again. Not in my studio alone, but onstage for all the world to see."

"Dancing is enough for you, then?"

No. Now that Hunter had come back into her life, dancing would never be enough.

"Dancing will be enough," she said.

"Mining diamonds will not be enough for me, Kathleen. My passion demands a partner."

She hated them all, the women who had already been his partners and the ones who would come after she left.

"You won't have any trouble finding one, Hunter. Good luck."

Her foot was on the top step when he stopped her again. The steely command in his voice was impossible to ignore.

"It's not my pity you should worry about, Kathleen. It's your own."

"I don't pity myself."

"Don't you? Then why are you running away, if not out of self-pity?" She put up a hand to stop him, but Hunter was relentless. "It's not loss of vision you need to worry about, but loss of spirit."

"How dare you . . ." She drew back and swung her fist just the way he'd taught her. She felt the jolt as it connected with his midriff.

"I dare that. And more." She swung at him with both fists. "Hit me, Kat. Show some fighting spirit."

She pommeled with the same single-minded vengeance she used to attack her dancing problems. Sweat beaded her upper lip and her hat fell to the floor. Still she battered at him.

"Damn you, Hunter . . . damn you . . . damn you."

Finally she sagged, all the fight gone. Hunter gathered her in his arms and drew her close.

"You don't need to fight me, Kat. I'm not the enemy."

"I know." She rested her head against his chest. "You may be the only true friend I ever had."

"Let me be your friend again, Kat."

She wrapped her arms around him, drawing on his good solid strength.

"If you will let me be yours." She lifted her face, and in her mind she could see him gazing down at her. She knew exactly how his eyes would look, how he would hold his mouth. "You've done all the giving, Hunter. There can be no true friendship without reciprocity. I *won't* be a charity case."

"You were never a charity case."

"But it was all one-sided. I had all the problems and you had all the solutions."

"God knows, I have problems."

"Then let me help you."

"You already have. More than you'll know." He kissed the top of her head. "You're balm to my weary soul, Kat. You're a taste of heaven for a man who has been in hell."

"Have you been in hell, Hunter?"

"Yes. A thirteen-year hell without you. I won't leave you again, Kat. You need to understand that."

Another stalemate. Kathleen remembered the weeks she'd lain in a hospital bed, battered, deaf, blind—and planning her comeback. She *would* return to the stage again. But what was a career without Hunter? Was it possible to have it all? And did she have the courage to try?

If she didn't, she'd always wonder. She reached out into the perpetual darkness and felt the sure, strong grip of Hunter's hand.

"Suppose I go with you?" she said.

"To Africa?"

"Don't you have a house there?"

"I have a whole damned compound. You can have a state-of-the-art dance studio with round-the-clock security. There will be no need to wear veils and mustaches." Suddenly he scooped her into his arms, whooping with joy. "You're brilliant, Miss Shaw. Did I ever tell you that?"

"Extraordinarily brilliant, I'd say."

"So would I."

He came to a halt and perched her on the edge of the kitchen counter. She wrapped her arms and legs around him.

"I'm scared, Hunter."

"Only fools are never scared." He kissed her eyes, her cheekbones, her jaw, the base of her throat. "There's no fear big enough that the two of us can't conquer. Africa is nothing to be afraid of."

It was not Africa she was afraid of.

"Hunter." She said his name again because the sound of it somehow reassured her. His hands whispered along the front of her silk blouse, and she felt the slow uncoiling of desire. She reached for his zipper. "Make love to me, Hunter."

He slid into her, and she lost herself in that swift hot joining. Reason departed. For Kathleen there was nothing except the reality of Hunter and the smooth hard surface of the Formica underneath her naked thighs.

EIGHT

"Kat, I want you to pack a bag with enough clothes to last a few days."

"A few days?" She straightened her clothes and slid off the Formica countertop. "Hunter, when I said I'd go to Africa with you, I didn't mean for a brief holiday. I meant for the duration. I won't be treated like a helpless child."

"Who said anything about Africa?"

"*I* did. That's the plan. We go to Africa to see if this man is your father."

"Not yet. There's a promise I have to keep before we go."

Before it's too late. The afterthought, coming to him so suddenly in the kitchen where they'd just made sweet, desperate love was a cold wind blowing down his spine.

Hunter was a self-made man, not one to pay attention to superstition; but what he felt was stronger than superstition, stronger than the notion that history was bound to repeat itself. He felt a dark power flowing across the ocean, waiting to suck them all under.

"Hunter?" Kathleen reached out and clutched his lapels, bringing his face close to hers. "What is this darkness that's sweeping over my soul?"

He wanted to rip the black thoughts from his mind and cast them into the river. But even then, Kat would find them. He could hide nothing from her.

"Shhh." He caught her fiercely to his chest. "There's no darkness, Kat. There's just you and me."

And a man called Tokolosh.

Africa loomed in his mind once more, dark and forbidding. His sense of foreboding swept through Kathleen like storm winds, and she trembled in his arms. There was only one way to hold back the fear.

Her lips were sweet and hot, and she tangled her hands in his hair and pulled him down to her, pulled him down to the floor.

"Don't be gentle," she whispered.

Every instinct he had told him that he no longer needed to chase after an elusive father, that everything he needed and wanted was lying beside him on the kitchen floor tenderly pushing his wild hair back from his damp face. But he was committed. Africa waited, and soon he'd make the journey.

Soon. Until then, there was Kathleen in this special secret place beside the river.

"Hunter?"

"What, love?"

"What is the promise you have to keep before we go?"

He kissed the beautiful eyes that could no longer see.

"To set you free."

"Mr. La Farge has explained your need for anonymity."

Kathleen felt like a thief in her boy's clothes and her scratchy mustache, as if she were taking something under false pretenses. But the man speaking to her allayed her fears.

"I can assure you we respect your privacy. There's no need for us to know your real name. Certainly you qualify. After you meet Jake and we're satisfied that the two of you can work effectively as a team, then you're all set."

"Thank you," she said.

"Are you ready?"

"Yes."

Mr. James Johnson of Rochester, Michigan, extended his arm. He'd been specific about the terms of their agreement. At her initial meeting with Jake, there would be just the two of them. They were to be a team, and the presence of someone else would merely be confusing.

"I think it's only fair to tell you that Jake has earned himself a reputation for being difficult. He's intelligent and knows this job as well as anyone here, but he's rejected everyone we've tried to pair him with. He has a mind of his own."

"So do I," Kathleen said.

"That's what Mr. La Farge tells me."

"Exactly what did Mr. La Farge tell you?"

"He said that you're headstrong and high-spirited."

"I might just kill him when I see him."

Mr. Johnson laughed. "He said you'd say that. I think you and Jake will make a great team. He needs a strong hand."

They were in a concrete corridor. Their shoes sounded hollow on the floor, and the coolness of the thick walls permeated her skin.

"Here we are." Mr. Johnson released her, and she heard the click of a latch. "Jake, come and meet your new mistress."

There was barely a sound as Jake approached her. She felt him stop a few inches away. What if he didn't like her? What if she didn't meet his rigid standards?

With one hand on her locket, she tried to still her panic. She mustn't let it show.

"Hello, Jake," she said.

Silence. Her heart thumped against her ribs and sweat beaded her upper lip.

"They say you're difficult," she said. "I've been called the same thing."

Difficult. Demanding. A perfectionist.

She'd heard some of the world's greatest choreographers speak of her in those terms . . . but always with respect, for they understood that her demands were not for herself but for ballet. The dance was everything, and she'd use every resource at her command to make it transcendent for the people who paid to watch.

"I think we can work together well, Jake. I'll give you a chance if you'll give me one."

There were the soft, almost silent steps as he moved closer. Then she felt his cold nose against her palm. He paused, sniffing, judging, making his decision. Suddenly the tail wagged, brushing against her leg.

"Well," Mr. Johnson said, obviously pleased. "It looks as if you've got yourself a guide dog."

There was no reason for Hunter to be terrified. But he was. Standing in his backyard watching Kathleen prepare to take her first outing with her guide dog simply terrified him.

Not that he didn't trust Jake. He was a smart gutsy German shepherd with an intense loyalty to his new mistress. The days they'd spent training together in Rochester had solidified a bond that Kat said had been almost instant between them.

"We're both mavericks," she'd told Hunter, laughing. "Headstrong and high-spirited. Together we'll scare the hell out of anybody who dares to get smart with us. And that includes you, Hunter La Farge."

Now, standing in his harness waiting for Kathleen's command, Jake gave every indication that what she'd said was true. He had that don't-tread-on-me look about him that should have set Hunter's heart at ease.

But it didn't. He supposed nothing would ever set his heart at ease where Kathleen was concerned. Somewhere deep inside him was the fear that at any moment she would be snatched from him once more, and he'd never find her again.

"Be careful, Kathleen."

"I'm only going to the French Quarter. You act as if I'm going to the moon." She reached up to adjust her mustache. "How do I look?"

"Like a cocky young man with one hell of a mean dog."

"Good." She leaned down and gave Jake a quick hug. "It's just you and me, boy." Then she thrust out her chin and got a good grip on the harness. "Jake. Forward."

They were off. Hunter resisted the urge to follow them. He'd promised Kat freedom, and he could not go back on his word.

Ah, Romance...

Don't you just *love* being in love? And what could be more
romantic than you and your special someone sunning on the beach
in exotic Hawaii, holding hands, listening to the pounding surf... or
strolling arm and arm around London, hearing Big Ben strike midnight
as you toast each other with champagne... or slipping out of a casino
to walk along the silky beaches of the Caribbean on a warm,
moonlit night? Sounds wonderful, doesn't it?

WIN A ROMANTIC INTERLUDE
AND $5,000.00 CASH!

What's even *more* wonderful is that **you could win** one of these
romantic **14-day vacations for two**, plus **$5,000.00 CASH**, in the
Winners Classic Sweepstakes! To enter, just affix the vacation sticker
of your choice to your Official Entry Form and drop it in the mail.
It costs you nothing to enter (we even pay postage!) — so *go for it!*

FREE GIFTS!

We've got **four FREE Loveswept Romances** and a **FREE Lighted Makeup
Case** ready to send to you, too!

If you affix the FREE GIFTS sticker to your Entry Form, four fabulous Loveswept
Romances are yours absolutely FREE. Plus, about once a month, you'll get four
new books hot off the presses, *before they're available in bookstores*. You'll always
have 15 days to decide whether to keep any shipment, for our low regular price,
currently just $11.95*. **You are never obligated to keep any shipment**, and
may cancel at any time by writing "cancel" across our invoice and returning the
shipment to us, at our expense. There's **no risk** and **no obligation** to buy, ever.

Now that's a pretty sweet offer, I think you'll agree—but we've made it even
sweeter! We'll also send you the **Lighted Makeup Case with mirror** shown on
the other side of this card—**absolutely FREE!** It has an elegant tortoise-shell
finish, and comes with an assortment of brushes for eye shadow, blush and lip
color. And the lighted mirror makes sure your look is always *perfect!*

**BOTH GIFTS ARE ABSOLUTELY FREE AND ARE YOURS TO KEEP
FREE FOREVER,** no matter what you decide about future shipments. So come on!
You risk nothing at all—and you stand to gain a world of sizzling romance,
exciting prizes ... and FREE GIFTS!

*(plus shipping & handling, and sales tax in NY and Canada)

Don't miss out! It's **FREE** to enter
our sweepstakes ... FOUR Romance novels are yours
FREE ... and the lighted makeup case is **FREE!**
You have nothing to lose — so enter today.

Good luck!

He shaded his eyes against the sun and watched until they were out of sight; then he looked at his watch and began to count the minutes.

It was going to be a very long day.

Did her terror show? Kathleen tamped it down. It wouldn't do to communicate fear to Jake. He was the guide dog, but she was the one in charge.

Freedom, Hunter had said. Where was the freedom of striking off in the damnable darkness hanging on to a harness and feeling the pull of an eighty-pound dog?

The pavement seemed to fly beneath her feet. All her senses had deserted her. She could feel neither buildings nor telephone poles. For all she knew, she could have been in Russia or China instead of walking down the streets of her neighborhood in Jefferson Parish.

Suddenly Jake stopped. They were at a curb, and he was waiting for her command. Oh, God, what if she sent him off against the light in the middle of traffic? All her weeks of dance training would be meaningless if she had two broken legs.

Jake nudged her leg. *The decision is yours*, he was saying.

Kathleen drew a deep breath and listened. The traffic assaulted her ears. Was the flow in front of her or to the side? She felt Jake's cold nose nudging against her hand.

"Everything's going to be all right, boy," she said. And suddenly she believed it. The traffic was clearly to her side.

"Forward," she said, and felt the pull of the harness as Jake stepped off the curb.

Other people were walking with her. She could hear their footsteps. The harness tugged upward, and she was across the street, standing safely on the other side.

Exhilaration filled her.

"Good boy," she said, bending down to hug her dog. "We did it, Jake. We did it!"

Jake licked the salty tears off her face, then Kathleen stood up and gave the command to go forward. A mockingbird in a nearby tree sang his summer song and a small dog in a nearby yard yapped a greeting to Jake. An old man with a quavery voice called out, "How you doing, pal?"

"Great," she said in her best manly voice.

"It's a fine day, ain't it?"

"It's a wonderful day!"

Quite suddenly she knew that it was. With a jaunty step she walked down the street, free at last.

Hunter paced his kitchen floor, and when he thought he might wear holes in the already worn linoleum, he went into the backyard and made a new path in the grass. By two o'clock in the afternoon, he was certain Kathleen had been kidnapped. By three, he was ready to go after her. By four, he came close to calling the police.

"Hunter. Are you there?"

He spun around, and there she was, her face aglow with excitement and her eyes filled with laughter.

"I'm here. Under the tree. How was your day, Kathleen?" Any fool could see.

"Magnificent. Perfect. And yours?"

"Great."

"You didn't worry about me?"

"Not for a minute."

Smiling, Kathleen unhooked Jake's harness then walked toward Hunter, stripping off her mustache as she went. He met her in the middle of the yard and guided her the last few steps to the tree. Softly she touched his face.

"Liar," she whispered.

"You know me too well."

She wound herself around him. "I'm going to know you better."

"In front of Jake?"

"He can close his eyes."

When her lips touched his, Hunter forgot everything except joy.

NINE

Kathleen felt the powerful throb of engines as Hunter's Learjet taxied down the runway and lifted into the sky. Jake lay calmly at her feet, and across the aisle Martha's knitting needles clicked so fast, she wondered that Martha didn't start a fire. Rick was spread out somewhere in front of her, his loud snoring evidence of two weeks of late-night debauchery.

Hunter reached for her hand.

"Scared?"

"No."

She was lying. Somewhere below them was security and safety. In two small cottages beside a moss-draped live-oak tree on a broken-down street, they had kept the rest of the world at bay. For a short time she and Hunter had recaptured the wild passion and sweet dreams of their youth. And now they were traveling into the unknown, speeding toward the dark continent that had once swallowed him up and left her with nothing except a stack of letters, a gold locket, and a broken promise.

Oh, yes indeed, she was scared. But she was never going to show it.

Tokolosh was sitting in the back of a run-down bar with his hat pulled low over his face when he got word that Hunter La Farge was back in Africa.

"Brought an old lady, a young boy, and a big dog with him." Tokolosh's informant spat on the floor, then wiped tobacco juice off his chin with the back of his hand. "Came in two weeks ago on that Learjet of his and been holed up in his compound ever since."

It was not like La Farge to be a hermit.

"He hasn't even been to his diamond mines?"

"Nobody's seen him. Been a bunch of trucks coming and going on the compound. Sounds of carpentry. Looks like he's building something."

"Adding on to his house?"

"Don't know."

"He was told about me?"

"Yes. He was told."

"When?"

"Four weeks ago when the foreman booked a flight to New Orleans."

Tokolosh pulled a handful of dirty bills out of his pocket and handed them to the man.

"You want me to do some more snooping, Tokolosh?"

"No. Your job's over. The rest is up to me."

He sat nursing his whiskey for a long time after the man had gone. Who were all those people La Farge had brought into his compound? And why hadn't he sent detectives sniffing around?

Tokolosh took a long pull on his bottle. His money was about to run out, and he was too damned old to hustle up some more.

When he stood up, the whiskey bottle rolled off the table and shattered on the floor. Cocking his hat at a jaunty angle, Tokolosh maneuvered around the broken glass. It would probably be there the next time he came.

If there was a next time.

"You leaving, Tokolosh?" the bartender called after him.

"Yep. Time to move on."

He had a son to claim—a son worth his weight in diamonds.

There was no need to wear her disguise on Hunter's compound. It was as secure and tightly guarded as Fort Knox.

Holding on to Jake's harness, Kathleen walked around the grounds, determined to learn them as well as she knew the small path that led from her cottage to Hunter's in Jefferson Parish.

"Tell me everything, Martha. I don't want you to leave out a thing."

In the distance came the sound of carpentry and Hunter's staccato commands. He was working three crews night and day to complete a studio for her, overseeing every detail himself.

"There's a giant baobab tree on your right. If you get too close, you're likely to trip."

"No. Especially not with Jake." She paused. "What's that noise I hear?"

"A bird."

"What kind? What does it look like?"

"A sugarbird. It's brown with a streak of yellow on its breast. The tail is long, kind of like a parrot's tail."

"What's that smell?"

"Flowers. Flame lilies."

"Red?" Kathleen laughed at herself playing detective. "Right?"

"Yes. You keep this up, and I'll be redundant."

"You'll never be redundant, Martha. You have a job with me as long as you want to stay."

"What about Hunter?"

Hunter's voice drifted across the compound. Kathleen felt it slide under her skin and spread throughout her body, the richness and wonder of it simply taking her breath away.

What about Hunter?

Every night he slid into her bed and she drew him deep into her body. And while the waves of passion swept over them they were safe. When morning came, he was gone.

If only morning would never come. But it always did. Always would.

"I can't stay here forever," Kathleen said.

"I'd like to know why not?"

"I must return to the stage."

"Whoever said you couldn't have it all? Is there some rule I don't know about? Whoever said you have to sacrifice a man like Hunter La Farge for a career?"

Kathleen was tempted to evade, but Martha, who was faithful and just and kind, deserved the truth.

"I can only handle one impossible dream at a time. And until I can prove myself on the stage, I will never consider being a part of Hunter's life."

"He would spit nails to hear you say that."

"I know how to dodge."

Kathleen gave the command, and Jake moved forward. She felt the presence of something, a tree perhaps, so like the live oak in Jefferson Parish that for a moment she was caught off guard.

"What is it, Martha?"

"A kippersol. Called a parasol tree."

"I think I'll sit under it for a while. You can go back to the house."

"And leave you here?" Martha sounded as if Kathleen had suggested she be turned over to cutthroats and thieves.

"I'll be perfectly fine. Jake and I know the way back. Besides, I need to be alone."

"Well . . . I'm not too sure."

"Remember the rule, Martha?"

"Don't hover. I know, I know. But I don't have to like it. You won't stay too long? This compound is huge, and I don't want Hunter to worry."

"He's busy with the carpenters."

"Hunter La Farge has eyes in the back of his head. He knows every move you make."

"Then I'd better familiarize him with the rule."

"Call me when you get ready to tell him. I want to see the fireworks."

"Scoot, Martha."

"I'm going . . . I'm going."

The sound of Martha's footsteps died away and there was nothing except the soft breeze whispering through the parasol tree, the call of the sugarbird, and the distant sound of hammering. Kathleen unharnessed Jake and stood with her face lifted to the sun.

Something stirred in her, and she knew that soon she would be dancing again, not in a studio hidden from the world, but onstage, with lights beaming down and the music of Tchaikovsky swirling around her. What would happen then? Would success separate her from Hunter once more or unite them forever?

A sudden chill shook her, and she wrapped her arms around herself to keep from shivering. The thought of losing Hunter was enough to bow her to the ground. Never to be in his arms again would be torture. Never to kiss him would be sheer agony. Never to feel him inside her would be a hell beyond bearing.

Almost she was tempted to ditch her dreams. Almost she was tempted to hide in his compound forever, going to sleep each night in his sweet, torturous embrace and waking each morning to feel his lips upon hers.

The chill shook her again, and she heard Jake growl, low in his throat. She lifted her head like a startled doe.

Someone was watching. She could feel the eyes upon her, not curious but cold, flat, deadly.

"Jake."

His response was immediate. She reached down and felt the raised hackles along his back. They were a long way from the house, and the pathway back was exposed. The sense of evil wafted over her, and she shivered once more. Jake still had his hackles up, but he was no longer growling. Surely he would be growling if the person were close.

"I must not panic," she whispered.

The parasol tree beckoned.

"Forward, Jake," she said.

The spreading branches closed around her, and she felt safe. No prying eyes could reach her under the tree. Sliding to the ground, she leaned against the trunk and pulled her dog close.

"Good boy," she said. "Good boy."

Breezes sighed around her, and the song of the sugarbird gave lie to her fears. How could harm come in a place of such tranquillity? How could evil penetrate the wall and the forces that guarded it?

Still, Kathleen waited. There was a tension in Jake as if he, too, were waiting, waiting and watching.

For the first time in weeks Kathleen cursed the darkness. Inwardly she railed against the bitter twist of fate that had taken her sight. To cower under a tree like a trapped animal. To sit with clenched fists listening for an enemy she couldn't see. It was a hell that almost sent her, keening, to her knees.

The thick branches let in no sun, and without it, Kathleen lost track of time. She'd foolishly left her braille watch on the bedside table, though what good a braille watch would do in her present situation was a mystery to her.

Jake growled low in his throat once more, and Kathleen put her hand on his head.

"Steady, boy. Everything is going to be all right."

She wished she believed it.

Nothing was visible through the binoculars except the thick branches of the parasol tree.

"Damn."

Tokolosh capped the binoculars and rocked back on his heels, thinking. The young boy was not a boy at all but a woman. And a beautiful one at that. Now, why in the world would La Farge have brought back a woman from the United States and then have kept himself holed up in his compound for two weeks? There was only one answer, and it made Tokolosh chuckle.

Once, long ago, a woman had turned his head and robbed him of all his senses. Fortunately he'd regained them before it was too late.

Thinking of the woman under the parasol tree, Tokolosh laughed again.

At last he'd found La Farge's Achilles' heel. He slung the binoculars around his neck and slipped down from the tree as easily as a snake.

"There's more than one way to skin a cat," he said.

It was dark when Hunter left the building site. The second crew had left and the third had just come in. Two more days, three at best, and the studio would be finished. Then Kathleen could dance again, dance until she was strong and confident, dance until a studio hidden in the bowels of Africa would not be enough for her.

Hunter rammed his fists into his pockets, trying not to think what would happen then. For now he had Kathleen, and that's all that mattered to him.

Flame flowers scented the night air and the sugarbird called to him as he made his way up the path to his house. She would be waiting for him, wearing one of the flowing, feminine dresses that swirled around her legs and emphasized her small waist.

"Kathleen." He stepped into the hallway, calling her name, lifting his head to catch the scent of gardenia.

"Hunter?" Martha peered around the door leading into a small sun room. Her face was puckered with worry and her eyes were too bright.

"Where's Kathleen?"

"I thought she'd be with you."

Fear climbed down Hunter's spine. He tried to keep it out of his voice.

"No. She's not with me. I just got back from the building site."

"I thought she might have gone there. . . . She's been gone so long."

Hunter felt chilled all the way to his bones.

"Gone where, Martha?"

"We walked. She said she wanted to be alone for a while, so I left her." She clutched the front of her dress. "If anything has happened to her, I'll just die."

"Nothing is going to happen to her." His voice lashed out like a whip.

Martha clutched the front of her dress. "Oh, Lordy, I didn't mean to upset you."

"And I didn't mean to upset you." He went to her and put a comforting hand on her arm. "Where did you leave her, Martha?"

"Under the parasol tree . . . on the south-west side of the compound."

"Is Jake with her?"

"Yes."

"Then there is absolutely nothing to worry about."

As he raced across the compound he prayed that he was telling the truth.

Kathleen had lost track of time. All she knew was that her legs were cramped and she was hungry. She had to get up enough nerve to leave the safety of the tree. Her hand tightened on Jake's harness.

"Ready, boy?" she said. Instantly she felt him go on the alert.

She was poised to go when she heard the footsteps, pounding as hard as native drums. Her heart flew to her throat.

"Kathleen!"

It was Hunter's voice, a beacon of safety and hope in the darkness. Relief made her weak. She sank back under the tree, and suddenly he was there, kneeling beside her, taking her into his arms.

"Hunter . . . oh, Hunter." She clung to his lapels.

"You're shivering." His hands were strong and soothing, moving softly across her back and down the length of her arms. He laced his fingers tightly with hers. "Tell me what happened."

"Nothing. I'm being a silly coward."

"You're neither silly nor a coward. Tell me, Kat."

"I thought I felt someone watching."

A dreadful sense of foreboding filled Hunter. With the instincts he'd developed from years of depending on his brain and his skills of survival, he understood his enemy. There was only one man who would watch. Only one man who would wait.

"What about Jake?" he asked.

"His hackles were up and he was growling. After we got under the tree, everything seemed to be all right. . . . I'm absolutely fine, Hunter. There's no need to hover."

"Dammit, Kat. I'm not hovering."

"Yes, you are. I'm perfectly capable of finding my way back to the house."

Hunter drew on all his willpower to keep from lifting Kathleen into his arms, taking her to the house, and keeping her under lock and key. He didn't think he could live if anything happened to her.

But instinct and long association with Kathleen Shaw told him the surest way to lose her was to try too hard to keep her.

"Of course you are. But it's far more fun with a companion."

The tension drained out of her body, just as he'd hoped it would.

"A companion?"

He loved the teasing note in her voice, the way she cocked her head and jutted out her chin. There was no power on earth that could take away her spirit. And if anybody tried, he would have to answer to Hunter La Farge.

"A friend?" he said, teasing her back.

"How about a lover?" she whispered.

She raked her fingernails down the front of his shirt, pausing at every button to slip them inside and caress his bare skin. Such a simple touch, and yet she might as well have been goading him with hot irons.

"You're playing with fire, my love."

"I know," she whispered, sighing. "I guess I'm destined to live dangerously."

Though he knew his compound like the back of his hand, he studied his surroundings, barely visible in the dark. They were in a small cul-de-sac, separated from the house and the eyes of the guards by a large stand of baobab trees. He glanced up at the overhanging branches of the parasol tree. With an addition of Spanish moss, it could be their tree in Jefferson Parish.

"Just how dangerous do you want to get?" he asked, reaching for her, touching her softly on the cheek.

"Very." She leaned her face into his warm palm. "Jake, go home."

The big dog padded off. From somewhere in the distance the sugarbird called again, and night came down softly around them.

Passion seized them as suddenly as a tropical storm, shaking them in its powerful grip. Braced against the tree, they both clung to each other, gasping.

"Nothing will ever take you from me again, Kat. Do you hear me? *Nothing.*"

"Please, Hunter . . . *Please.*"

He knew what she wanted, what they both wanted, what they both needed. And so began the tumultuous journey that wiped everything else from their minds.

Almost.

Somewhere on the other side of the wall was the man who had led him through the jungles and over the mountains for years, the man who had haunted his dreams and excited his imagination. Somewhere on the other side of the wall was the man who called himself Hunter's father.

Soon Hunter would have to face him.

Kathleen called out to him in a voice tight with passion. Volcanoes exploded in him, and hurricanes raged with a force that almost sent him to his knees.

Too soon he'd have to leave, but not yet. Not yet.

For a while there was only Kathleen. He knelt to the ground, taking her with him. Then slowly, like some fine animal from the jungle, he feasted.

TEN

As soon as Hunter had Kathleen safely back at the house, he left and called the head of his security into his office.

"Double the guards around the compound, Tubu."

"Reason?" Tubu was a man of few words.

"Someone is watching Kathleen."

"Consider it done. Do we know who?"

"Tokolosh," Hunter said, following his gut instinct. "He's ready to be found. Find him."

"And?"

"Here is what you are to do."

Hunter issued rapid-fire instructions, and after Tubu left, he stood looking across the compound to the studio. Although it had been under construction only two weeks, already it looked as if it had sprung up naturally among the parasol trees. Soon it would be finished. Soon he'd have no more excuses to stay on the compound.

Through the open windows he could hear music. Kathleen was never without it. When he'd left her, she was headed to the bath. He pictured her now, standing naked with the water and the music cascading around her, each movement of her arms as graceful as if she were onstage.

Filled with purpose, he strode to the studio and sent away the night crew.

In the days that followed, he found flaws with the already completed work. The floors had to be redone. And the mirrors. The sound system wasn't perfect and had to be sent back and another ordered.

Kathleen brought him to task. Sitting in the middle of his carved bed with her hair tumbled across her naked breasts and the mosquito netting swaying behind her in the breezes from the window, she looked like an exotic princess.

"Last week you told me the studio was almost finished," she said.

"Things went wrong."

"You're stalling."

"It has to be perfect."

Kathleen went absolutely still. The moon moved from behind a cloud and washed her in silvery light. She looked ephemeral, as if she had already vanished and become a figment of his dreams.

Desperate, he pulled her on top of him and held her fiercely to his chest.

"We can't hold back time like this forever," she whispered.

"We can try."

"Yes, my love," she whispered. "We can try."

Tokolosh had misjudged his son.

When word came from Hunter La Farge, it came through an emissary, and not even his right-hand man, but someone of such low rank that Tokolosh was insulted. He took great pains not to let his true feelings show. Sitting in a hotel room he'd rented for the occasion and wearing a suit he'd bought at a secondhand shop, he tried to look like a man of means instead of a down-and-out vagabond with no place to go and no money to take him there.

"Mr. La Farge requests blood tests before he will agree to meet with you. I've brought his personal physician with me."

The man speaking to him with such arrogance had merely introduced himself as Tubu. He had the sleek, dangerous look of a panther that suggested he might be a bodyguard. His black hair was pulled back with a leather thong and the crease in his khaki shorts was so sharp, it looked as if it would cut paper.

Tokolosh wanted to tell Tubu what he could

do with his personal physician, but for once in his life he used restraint. His goal was to get to Hunter La Farge, not instant gratification.

"Certainly," he said, rolling up his sleeve. "Anything to get me an audience with my son." *An audience*. As if Hunter La Farge were the pope. He'd chosen his words deliberately in order to convey just the right mix of eagerness and respect.

The needle was relatively painless. While the personal physician filled a vial with dark red blood, Tubu stood at the window looking out as if he had no interest in the proceedings. Suddenly he whirled around, his voice cracking like a whip.

"Mr. La Farge would like to know your last name."

"Tell La Farge he'll find out when he asks the question in person." Tokolosh nailed the man with his blue eyes. "Not before."

Tubu took a while deciding whether to press the issue. In the end, he headed for the door.

"You'll hear from Mr. La Farge," he said when his hand was on the knob.

Tokolosh had too much class to ask when. Let the arrogant son of a bitch think he had money to burn, staying in the most expensive hotel in the city with room service every day.

"Tell my son I look forward to meeting him at last."

❖————————————————❖

Hunter had designed his office to give the feeling that he was outdoors among exotic plants and cool trees instead of barricaded in a compound with enough guards to provide security for a head of state. Part of the reason for the design was a reaction against his early years in Africa when he'd spent hours and days and months in the darkest reaches of the earth, searching for diamonds. The total absence of light had affected him in ways he hadn't even realized until he'd started building his house and his offices.

The first plan, drawn by a renowned architect, featured high walls with narrow windows just below the ceiling. There was enough light, but the walls made it impossible to see the trees. Hunter had thrown the plans in the garbage can and drawn his own.

It was one of the many ways he'd earned the reputation of being a tyrant. He was called other names as well. Dangerous, daring, cynical, heartless, cold. He'd earned them all. The names had fit . . . before Kathleen had returned.

Now, sitting behind his massive teakwood desk, he hoped that Tokolosh had heard of his reputation. When he faced the adventurer who called himself his father, Hunter wanted to be on even ground.

The intercom buzzed, and his secretary announced Dr. William Reich. As usual, Hunter's physician minced no words. With his long frame twisted into the chair like a pretzel, he folded his narrow hands into a steeple and stared at a spot just beyond Hunter's head.

"As you know, these tests can't prove conclusively that this man is your father, only that he is not." Hunter tensed. "The blood tests show that this man *could* be your father."

Hunter was unprepared for the sense of elation that caught him. After so many years he'd thought himself immune to the old dreams.

"Anything else?" he asked.

"Blood-alcohol content was high."

"He's an alcoholic?"

"He'd been drinking heavily. That proves nothing. Maybe he was nervous about the prospect of meeting you." William unfolded his hand, focused on Hunter's face, and gave him a boyish grin. "Hell, I was nervous about meeting you the first time. From all the rumors, I guessed you'd be a cross between King Kong and King Henry the Eighth."

"And?"

"You didn't disappoint me." He unsnapped his medical bag and handed the test results to Hunter. "You can look these over at your leisure. If you have any questions, just call me."

"Thanks, William." Hunter left his desk and

shook the doctor's hand. "You've done your usual excellent job."

"I'm the best. That's why I charge you a fortune."

After William left, Hunter stared down at the test results, not seeing them at all, but seeing the months and years he'd roamed Africa searching for this man. After all those years of playing elusive games, why had Tokolosh suddenly chosen to reveal himself?

There was only one motive Hunter could think of: money.

He struggled against the bitterness that curled like smoke inside him. If he weren't careful, the bitterness could consume him, could wipe out the last vestiges of the optimistic little boy who had wanted nothing except a father and a name.

"Hunter?"

Kathleen stood in the doorway with Jake at her side. An enormous silk scarf was knotted at her waist and swirled around her dance leotard.

"They said you'd be here. I hope I'm not interrupting."

"Never. You're exactly what I need." With one hand he pulled her close and with the other he shut the door.

Kathleen slid into his embrace, welcoming his lips with a wild abandon that quickly escalated out of control.

"I can never get enough to make up for all

the lost years." He pulled her hips hard against his rigid flesh. "Never."

"Hunter, I came to talk about important things."

"More important than this?" His lips seared the side of her neck. "And this?" He toyed with her nipple.

The sweet, hot swelling would not be denied. Quietly she took off Jake's harness and sent him off to play. Hunter drew her back inside and carried her across the room. He cleared his desk with one sweep of his arm, then spread her upon its smooth surface. The multicolored silk scarf spread around her like the petals of an exotic flower.

When he peeled away the silk and the leotard, she lay upon his dark desk like a carving of ivory. Braced on his elbows, he swept his gaze over her, memorizing each enticing curve, each seductive hollow. Chill bumps rose along her arms and across her abdomen.

She cupped her breasts and offered them up, a sacrifice to the god of passion. As his mouth closed over her nipple she pulled him fiercely down to her.

"We can't keep doing this, Hunter."

He knew what she was talking about. Not the loving, not the delicious mating that drugged the senses and filled the heart. But the postponement. Sheltered in his compound, locked in each other's embrace, they were postponing the time when both of them would have to face the real world.

He toyed with her nipple, hard as a diamond, then pulled her deep into his mouth. Euphoria stole over him, and desire bright and sharp as a sword sliced through him. Soon it would rip him asunder and he would be incapable of anything except burying the pieces of himself in her hot flesh and being made whole again.

He lifted his head while he could, then caught her face fiercely between his hands.

"There is nothing else but this, Kathleen. Nothing!"

He lowered himself until the velvety tip of his sex barely dipped into her soft, wet folds. She eased her hips upward, trembling.

"Only this," he whispered. "Now and forever."

The tremors that shook her felt like weeping. He braced her hips, holding her back, keeping her on the edge.

"We can't go on like this forever, Hunter."

"Tell me you don't want to."

"I want to, but—"

"Shhh . . ." He eased out and raked the tip of himself over her abdomen, moist as a kiss. "Do you trust me, Kat?"

Did she dare? Would he keep her like this forever, a prisoner of passion? The hot velvet skimmed over her skin once more. Sweet agony. Worth any price.

"No," she said with a moan. "I don't trust you for a minute."

"Yes, you do, Kat. You trust me." He dipped briefly inside her, then withdrew. "I'm your soul and you are mine."

Need screamed along her nerve endings and clawed at her belly. She could feel the glow from a fine sheen of sweat that covered her body.

"Yes . . . Hunter, yes . . . please."

He thrust once, impaling her. Her body arched like a bowstring, and she could feel the vibrations all the way down to the end of her toes.

"Now?" he whispered.

"Yes . . . now."

They were wild and savage, panting, their hot breaths mingling, their hearts pounding like native drums.

"Don't . . . ever . . . let . . . me . . . go." Her plea was ragged, coming out in gasps as they rode the waves of passion.

"Never." His hot breath seared the side of her throat as his body went rigid. "Never!" he whispered as thick hot juices flowed through her like lava.

They collapsed together, her legs twisted around his hips and his head resting in the curve of her shoulder. When their strength finally re-

turned, he lifted her off the desk and carried her
to the sofa. Then, kneeling beside her, he tenderly wiped away the sweat with her scarf. She
lay with her eyes closed, feeling the drift of silk
over her skin.

"You've made me forget there was ever anything except the two of us and this magnificent
obsession," she whispered.

"You call it obsession. I call it love."

She held him close, until the sun fell from
the sky and the stars came out and made silvery
patterns on their naked skin.

They had food and a bottle of champagne
delivered from his kitchen.

Lying back against the sofa cushions, they
fed each other, laughing and touching and kiss-
ing softly. Kathleen knew that in the weeks and
months to come she would always remember
them this way, full of each other, happy as children, oblivious to everything except the sensations that ignited like Fourth of July sparklers
between them.

She hated to be the one to break the spell.

"I called the other crews to come back to the
studio," she said.

He stiffened. Then setting the food aside, he
drew her into the circle of his arm and pressed
her head against his shoulder.

"We don't have to talk about this, Kat."

"Yes. We do." She eased out of his arms and braced herself against the end of the sofa. "The studio will be finished tomorrow."

There was a heavy silence. She wished she could see his face. Instead she had to rely on her senses, and what she felt was the tension in him, the denial.

"We can't go on this way forever," she said.

"I know."

"I have to dance."

"I know that too." He took her hand, kissed the palm. "I *want* you to dance. I want you to be at stage center with the eyes of the world upon you. I've always wanted you to have that dream . . . and I'll do everything in my power to make it come true. Do you believe me, Kat?"

"Yes, Hunter. I believe you."

"Six months from now you'll be in New York at Lincoln Center and I'll be in the front row seat, cheering my wife on."

His words sent shivers through her.

"Your wife?"

His laughter was rich and deep.

"Are you so surprised? We've always known it would be so."

"It's something I haven't thought about in a long time."

Hunter had always known her moods, and she felt his stillness now, his disbelief. Don't, she pleaded silently. Don't press the issue. Not now of all times.

As if he'd read her thoughts, he lifted her foot and planted a kiss in the arch. When he released her, his tone was light and beguiling.

"It's high time you started thinking about it again, Kathleen Shaw. I don't intend for you to be a kept woman the rest of your days."

"A kept woman?"

"Yes, indeed. A kept woman." He sucked her big toe.

"Ha." She jerked her foot away from him and stalked naked around his office, pretending a magnificent rage. "You call this being *kept*, Hunter La Farge? Where I come from, kept women are showered with jewels."

"I thought you'd rather be showered with something else."

She could hear the laughter bubbling up in his chest. That was good. If they laughed long enough, they might hold time suspended in this golden day filled with love.

"I haven't felt any showers lately. Not even the tiniest sprinkle."

"You haven't?" She heard him leave the sofa. Heard his footsteps as he stalked her.

"No. Not even a hint of a sprinkle."

He was closer now, so close she could feel his body heat. Passion surged through her. Standing naked and breathless, she glowed with it.

Silk whispered, and suddenly she felt the

scarf around her waist. Hunter tugged gently, drawing her forward.

"Come here, you insatiable wench."

"Not unless you make it worth my while."

The scarf tightened, pulling her closer, so close to the heat that she was melting.

"I intend to make it worth your while, all right." Another tug. The heat ripped through her so hard that she cried out. She heard the slosh of liquid being poured, then felt the tip of his finger against her taut nipple, wet and ripe with the smell of champagne.

"Very worth your while," he added, tugging at the scarf.

The silk landed at her feet, and they slid to the floor with it, already entangled, already lost.

ELEVEN

They didn't leave his office that night, and when morning came, Kathleen was curved softly against him on the sofa, sleeping. The sun coming through the parasol trees made lacy patterns on her skin. She stirred, sighing, then settled back against the cushions with one arm stretched over her head.

She sighed once more, smiling in her sleep. As Hunter watched her his heart ached. Today she would begin rehearsals in her newly completed studio, and in a few months, perhaps even a few weeks, she would be ready for the stage.

And then the small paradise they'd created would vanish . . . unless he could find a way to make it last forever.

Sliding quietly off the sofa, he went into the private dressing area adjoining his office to shower and put on fresh clothes. So he wouldn't wake Kathleen, he took his braillewriter into the dressing room. The note was brief, and he left it on top of her leotard beside the sofa. Then he covered her with a light afghan, slipped a stack of CDs on the player, and turned the volume down low.

Outside his office, his secretary was already at her desk. In her midforties, she had the look of a woman who could battle dragons and come out a winner. He had chosen her for the reasons he chose all his employees, because of her intelligence and her ability to keep her own counsel. She was loyal from the top of her head to the tips of her toes. Even if Hunter's personality hadn't inspired that kind of loyalty, the exorbitant salaries he paid guaranteed it.

"Laura Lee, Miss Shaw is in my office and is not to be disturbed. When she wakes up, see that breakfast is brought to her, then have someone bring Jake over."

"Certainly." Laura Lee made quick, precise notes. "Anything else?"

"I'm sending extra guards for the perimeters of this building, and when Miss Shaw leaves, they are to accompany her to the studio. I'll be back sometime tonight."

"Is there a number where you can be reached."

"No."

Laura Lee didn't blink an eye at that bit of information. She was accustomed to her boss leaving on the spur of the moment for places that didn't even have toilets, let alone telephones.

"Be careful, Hunter."

He laughed. "You always say that."

"That's because you're always going into places fraught with danger."

"Fraught? Now that's an old-fashioned word."

"I'm an old-fashioned woman. And if I may be so bold as to say so, I think Kathleen Shaw has been good for you. Softened your edges a bit. I hope she'll stay."

"I'm doing my damnedest to see that she does."

"Maybe I'll put in a good word for you while you're gone."

"Put in several."

Outside, the air was clear and sweet, filled with the song of the sugarbird and the fragrance of flowers. In the bright yellow glow of the sun, the compound looked peaceful, a paradise set apart from the rest of the dark continent. Hunter slipped on his sunglasses and looked upward where guards were posted around the top of the thick stucco walls. Their holstered guns were at odds with the birdsong and the gentle swaying of the parasol trees.

A vision of Kathleen lying naked on the sofa, dreaming, came to him swiftly.

"This time I won't let the music stop for you, my love."

With one last glimpse at the guards, he climbed into his Jeep and drove off to slay his demons.

When the phone call finally came, it took Tokolosh by surprise.

"Dammit all to everlasting hell," he muttered, placing the receiver back on the hook. "Bastard."

Walking on legs that felt wobbly from booze, he made his way to the bathroom. The sight in the mirror was not a pretty one. As a matter of fact, it was enough to scare women and frighten little children.

Cursing under his breath, he drew hot water and tried to make repairs. Even as he cursed he admired La Farge's tactics. Catch the enemy off guard. It was the first rule in jungle warfare.

As he scraped the straight-edged razor over his scraggly whiskers, he harbored no doubts about the imminent meeting with Hunter La Farge. It would be jungle warfare, a seasoned old lion being challenged by one full of the vigor and power of youth.

When he was satisfied that he'd done the best he could with his face, he slicked his gray hair back with water and tied it with a leather thong. Then he twisted his head to get a side view.

"Not bad for an old man," he said. Tokolosh could still set women's hearts aflutter.

Unexpectedly he thought of her, standing beside the river with the wind blowing her dress against her legs. She had tasted sweeter than any woman he'd ever known, like magnolia blossoms mixed with the rich dark molasses favored by her people.

Light from the naked bulb in the bathroom fell across his face and caught the glisten of tears. With a curse, he bent over the sink and dashed water on his face.

He could afford to show no weakness today.

She knew she was alone the minute she woke up. Kathleen felt the cushions anyhow, then called his name.

"Hunter?"

There was no answer. Only the hum of the air-conditioning and the gentle swell of music. She stretched, luxuriating in the heavy, sated feel of her body. If she let herself, she could stay forever in this sweet, secret prison.

She cast off the afghan Hunter had covered her with, then reached for her clothes. The note was on top. Quickly she ran her hands over the raised dots.

My love, I'll see you tonight.

No explanation. No signature.

Kathleen laid the note on the end table, then went into Hunter's shower and stood while the warm water rushed over her. Drawing the soapy washcloth over her body, she could feel the shape and tone of her muscles. Weeks of dancing had made her stronger. Excitement and energy surged through her.

When she was dressed, she snapped open her braille watch. Eleven o'clock. Almost half the day was gone already.

She hurried from the office.

"Miss Shaw?"

The voice belonged to Hunter's secretary.

"Please . . . call me Kathleen."

"I've ordered breakfast for you. After you eat, I'll send someone for Jake."

"Thank you, Laura Lee."

"Hunter's orders."

"Where is he?"

"I don't know Miss . . . Kathleen. He left early this morning and said he couldn't be reached."

Loss and something like panic filled Kathleen. Until that moment she hadn't realized how heavily she'd come to depend on Hunter. He was always nearby, always accessible. And the few times he'd left her side—in Jefferson Parish to take braille lessons or to do some small errand—he'd always told her where he would be. In fact he'd been meticulous about that.

"Trust me, Kat," he said. "I'll always be there for you."

Why hadn't he told her where he was going?

She reached out for something to touch, something to anchor her. Her hand closed over the back of a chair, and she drew in deep, steadying breaths.

"Are you all right?" Laura Lee's voice was filled with concern.

"Yes. I'm fine."

"Breakfast will be right up. I thought fresh fruit and croissants would be good."

"Thank you. That sounds wonderful."

Without Hunter, nothing sounded wonderful. Where was he?

Laura Lee served her breakfast on the glass table in the employees' lounge, where sun and birdsong poured through the open windows. Jake was brought in midway through the meal, and he rubbed against her legs, whining.

"It's okay, boy. Everything is all right."

But he knew that it wasn't. The mystical bond between them made it impossible for Kathleen to hide her true feelings from her guide dog. He sensed her turmoil, and although he didn't know its source, he empathized.

Sitting in the sun alone with her dog, Kathleen felt her blindness. It whispered around her like a dark ghost, beat through her like the wings of a raven.

She clenched her fists and lifted her chin.

"No," she whispered. "I will not give in to this weakness."

Jake thumped his tail against the floor, and she leaned down to pat his head.

"Come, boy, we have work to do."

Pushing her food aside, she caught his harness and left the room.

"Laura Lee, I'll be at the studio in case anyone asks."

"Kaliba and Bantu will go with you."

"Kaliba and Bantu?"

"Bodyguards."

Kathleen stiffened. "I don't need bodyguards."

"Those are Hunter's orders."

Kathleen would not argue and place Laura Lee in the position of disobeying her boss. Nor would she send Kaliba and Bantu away for the same reason.

She had the long walk to the studio and the rest of the day to think about what she would say to Hunter.

He hadn't expected to feel anything. Standing in the doorway of the hotel room staring at the tall man with the riveting blue eyes, Hunter felt a deep curiosity and a flutter of something that others might have called filial longings. He stoutly refused to acknowledge any such feelings, either by expression or gesture.

"Tokolosh," he said, moving into the room like a panther set to spring.

"Hunter La Farge." Tokolosh didn't offer his hand, didn't show by so much as a tic in his cheek that Hunter was more to him than a casual visitor.

The two men stood two feet apart, taking measure. Tokolosh was the first to fold. He averted his eyes from Hunter's fierce stare and sank onto the edge of the bed, leaving the chair for his guest.

In the game they were playing, it was a small triumph for Hunter. He straddled the chair, his eyes giving lie to his relaxed body.

"What do you want from me?" Hunter asked.

Tokolosh hadn't expected the blunt question. He considered making up a pretty lie, embroidering the truth with fiction about an old man's longings to see his son. But one look at Hunter's eyes stopped him.

"Money," he said.

"How much?"

"Enough to live comfortably the rest of my life." An old injury from a bad encounter with a rhino sometimes bothered him. Tokolosh shifted on the bed, trying to get more comfortable. "I'm broke and I'm too old to go out and try to make a living."

Hunter studied him in silence. Tokolosh sat still under the fierce inspection.

"Why should I give you money?"

"Because I'm your father."

Hunter didn't move, but his muscles tensed as if he were about to pounce.

"Who are you?" His voice cracked like a whip.

"Your father. Blood doesn't lie."

"It doesn't prove the truth, either."

Sweat inched down the side of Tokolosh's face and formed in wet circles under his arms. Hunter sat unmoving, only his black eyes alive. Something welled in the old man's chest, and if he hadn't known better, he'd have called it pride.

"Your mother was a beautiful woman." There was a low sound of protest from Hunter, like the growl of an angry animal. "When the freighter I was on steamed into port, she was standing on the bank of the river wearing a pink dress and a little corsage of violets. She'd just come from church."

Hunter's heart pounded so hard, he wondered that the other man couldn't hear. He'd seen that dress hanging in his mother's closet, the pink faded over the years and the little corsage of dead violets pinned in a plastic bag to keep the petals from shedding.

"Never underestimate the power of a churchgoing woman." Tokolosh had a faraway look on his face as if he'd traveled backward in time and left Hunter sitting alone in the hotel room. "Janice made me forget every other woman except her. Sweet. God, she was sweet. Had this little bitty heart-shaped birthmark inside her left elbow right where her pulse beat. I think it was the sight of that little beating heart that made me lose my senses."

Tokolosh sounded like a man deeply in love. Hunter hardened his heart. If Tokolosh had been so much in love, why had he left Hunter's mother pregnant with no money and no job? The question burned in his mind, but he didn't ask it. He wasn't ready to acknowledge that the man sitting on the bed had anything to do with him and his mother.

"That summer I spent with her was the happiest in my life. At night we used to sneak up onto the roof and lie naked on her grandmother's quilt, drinking cheap wine and counting the stars."

The quilt was a star-of-Texas pattern and still hung on the wall of Hunter's cottage in Jefferson Parish. Now he understood why his mother sometimes cried when she looked at it. Now he knew about the stain in the middle of the star.

Why? Why did you leave her?

He felt smothered, but he wouldn't show any sign of weakness by taking the deep breath he so needed.

"Who are you?" he asked, his voice harsh in

the stillness of the cramped room. "Who in the hell are you?"

Tokolosh left the bed and studied the view from the window.

"Mongo," he whispered. "The Black Knight. Tokolosh."

"Who *are* you?"

The old man turned around slowly. Backlit by the sunlight, he looked like one of the carved gods Hunter had seen in lost cities of the Congo.

"My name is Johnathan McFarland."

Tokolosh/Johnathan waited, still as a lion while the truth sank in. Hunter's hands closed around the top of the chair, squeezing so tightly, his knuckles turned white.

Johnathan McFarland. Thirty-year-old white male. Six-two. One hundred eighty-five pounds. Blue eyes. Black hair.

He'd seen the old posters in the post office. There had even been a television special once long ago.

Johnathan McFarland. Wanted for murder.

Kathleen wiped her face with a towel. The front of her leotard was soaked with sweat and her legs felt heavy. She was still out of shape. Two years earlier that much dancing wouldn't have disturbed a hair on her head, let alone cause her to break out in a sweat.

"You need anything, Miss Shaw?"

It was one of the bodyguards. She'd forgotten which one.

"No, thank you."

She flipped back the cover on her braille watch. Six P.M. Where in the world was Hunter?

She couldn't stand the thought of going back to the house and sitting at the dining table without him. She couldn't endure the thought of the lonely house, the lonely bed.

"Yes, on second thought. Could you call the kitchen and have them send me a sandwich. I think I'll take my dinner break here in the studio."

"Certainly. What kind?"

"Anything will do. Whatever they have."

What did it matter? Nothing would taste good without Hunter.

She resisted the urge to bury her face in her hands. One day without him and she was falling apart. What would happen to her when she had to spend days without him? Weeks? Months?

The thought filled her with stark terror. And it was then that she knew exactly what she had to do when Hunter returned.

She checked her watch once more. Where was he?

The money lay scattered on the floor. Occasionally a gust of air caught one of the bills and sent it fluttering upward like an awkward bird.

Johnathan squatted among the money, disbelief and rage warring in him. Every now and then he burst out with a new string of curse words.

All his years of running had come to this: crawling around on the floor like a dog picking up scraps tossed out by his son.

His son . . .

"Feel, Johnathan. Our son is already kicking."

He pressed his hands over Janice's flat abdomen, indulging her. There was no sign of life within, but he pretended to be pushed back by the vigorous kicking. Her quick laughter was his reward.

Spanning her tiny waist, he picked her up and spun her around and around.

"You're making me, dizzy, Johnathan."

"You make me dizzy . . . always have and always will." *He set her on the floor and kissed her soundly.* *"Tomorrow we'll get married."*

They had made frantic love on the smooth wooden floor with the old air conditioning laboring hard to cool the stifling apartment. He thought he'd burst with love.

That was the night he'd killed for her.

They had been in a small bar, celebrating. The man came out of nowhere while he'd gone to the bathroom, drunk, putting his hands all over Janice, telling her exactly what he was going to do to her, trying to drag her out into the alley.

In his red rage, Johnathan never remembered pulling the knife, only the blood and Janice screaming. Newspaper and television reporters called her the "unidentified woman" with descriptions ranging from tall and brunette to petite and blond. They didn't have the same trouble with him, however. They described him right down to the scar on his cheek.

"Run, Johnathan. You have to run."

"And hide like a dog?" Already he was hiding like a dog, standing in the alley behind a row of garbage cans, trying to protect Janice with his body. *"No. There has to be a way out."*

"There isn't. Don't you see? You're an out-of-work drifter. They'll send you to prison . . . or to the chair." She clutched the front of his shirt, sobbing. *"Oh, Johnathan. I'd die if anything happened to you."*

"What about the baby?"

Her chin came up. "Our son will be fine."

He tried to turn back time with his kiss, but in the distance the sirens were wailing.

"Go . . . hurry."

One last kiss. Desperate. Heartsick. Then he was racing down the alley. At the end, he turned to her.

"I'll send for you."

He never had. He'd meant to. But there was

always a reason not to—no money, no job, no place to live. Somehow the days had become months and the months had become years.

And then, when word drifted through Africa that Hunter La Farge, son of Janice Smith of Jefferson Parish was looking for his father, he'd been afraid, afraid to confront the son he'd tried to put out of his mind.

Scrabbling around on his hands and knees, he picked up the money. Probably several thousand dollars. Enough to pay off his hotel bill and rent a cheap room somewhere for a few months, buy some cheap whiskey.

"I have no father, and I won't be blackmailed," Hunter had said, tossing the money carelessly, as if it meant nothing to him. "Here. This is more than you ever did for me."

And then he'd walked out.

Johnathan's hands trembled as he stuffed the money into his pockets and headed out the door. There was nothing to pack except a toothbrush, and he didn't plan to be in any condition to brush his teeth for the next few weeks.

He paid off his bill, then headed down the street for the nearest liquor store. Armed with enough booze to keep him drunk for the next few days, he stepped out into the warm night and uncapped one of the bottles. No sense waiting.

The cheap liquor burned going down. He

took another long pull. Some of it dribbled down his chin and spilled on the front of his suit.

A scrawny cat ran out in front of him, and he turned into the alley where it had been hiding. He took off his jacket and fashioned a pillow for himself, then stretched out, carefully cradling the liquor.

Ironic that he'd ended up exactly where he left off almost thirty-two years ago. A vision of Janice came to him, standing in the alley waving good-bye.

I love you, Johnathan. I'll always love you.

"Here's to you, Janice, wherever you are." He lifted his head off the makeshift pillow so the booze wouldn't strangle him. "And to you, Hunter La Farge, King of Diamonds."

The bitter bile of defeat rose in his throat. Nothing in his life had ever turned out the way he'd thought it would. He judged the level of liquor in the bottle before he upended it once more.

You're a smart man, Tokolosh. Why don't you try to make something of yourself?

Marlin Lincoln, the only friend he'd ever had had told him that . . . how many years ago? Ten? Twelve?

Marlin had died the only way it was possible in the wilds of Africa, violently. Was that to be his fate too?

Suddenly Johnathan shivered. He'd imagined so much more for himself.

The liquor began to swirl around in his head, and out of the alcoholic fumes came a vision, a woman with long black hair sitting under the parasol tree with her dog. He stared at his bottle, seeking inspiration.

Perhaps there was a way out after all.

TWELVE

The lights were still on in the studio.

It was nearly midnight. He'd expected to find Kathleen in the bed, to slip in beside her and find sweet forgetfulness in her arms. No questions. No explanations. Just quick, desperate passion that burned away everything except the taste and smell and feel of her.

Hunter dismissed the two guards at the door, had them take Jake back to the house, then stood in the doorway watching. He didn't call her name, didn't move close. Like a long-lost soldier returning to his beloved homeland, he devoured every small detail of her, the dark curls that had escaped from her ponytail and were plastered to her cheeks with sweat, the slender hands that moved like two snow-white birds, the graceful throat where her pulse fluttered, the high proud thrust of her breasts.

Here was everything he needed, contained in the softness of woman, the passionate indomitable spirit of Kathleen. Nothing else mattered. Certainly not a brief encounter in a hotel room.

What do you want from me?

Money . . . money . . . money.

Hunter clenched his hands into fists to shut out the memory. What had he expected to find in that room? A father? At his age?

He bit back a harsh laugh. Music filled the room, music and the muffled sound of Kathleen's ballet slippers against the floor.

Suddenly he saw her with new eyes, not as the woman he loved but as a dancer. She was magnificent, transcendent. She whirled around the room without a bobble, finding her way through the darkness with a grace that took his breath away. Watching her, he would never have guessed that she couldn't see.

Leaning against the door, he watched until the music ended.

"*Brava!*" he said, clapping his hands. "*Brava!*"

She lifted her head like a doe caught in the woods by predators.

"Hunter . . ." She made no move to come toward him, but stood in the middle of the studio with a peculiar waiting stillness.

"You're ready for the stage, Kathleen."

"Not yet."

"You're magnificent."

"I have to be perfect."

Silence swirled around them. Her breasts rose and fell with her softly labored breathing. He started across the floor.

She didn't speak, didn't move as he approached her. He stopped only inches from her, surrounded by jasmine heated by her exertions and lying fragrant along her glowing skin. A small bead of sweat shiny as a star inched down the side of her neck and pooled in the spot where her pulse beat.

Careful not to touch her yet with his hands, he leaned forward and licked the moisture, sucking on her skin as if he could take her into himself and keep her there forever. A small tremor shook her, but she remained still and silent in the middle of the dance floor, a Venus carved in ivory.

Drunk with her, he reached up and untied the ribbon in her hair, holding out his hands so he could catch the silky strands as they cascaded around her shoulders. The rhythm of her breathing changed. His need became almost unbearable, but tonight he didn't want quick relief. He wanted to sink slowly into her and drown, spending hours, days, plunging so deep that there was nothing except sensation and oblivion.

Her hair clung to his fingers, curling intimately around them. With gentle pressure, he pulled her close. Hot. She was so hot. He pressed his aching body against hers, fitting himself between her legs. She sucked in her breath, once, sharply.

With his hands still in her hair, he gazed down at her. He could see each separate eyelash, the tiny line of moisture along her upper lip, the lips themselves, full, ripe, slightly parted.

Like dancers in an erotic tango, they swayed together, trapped by the dark music that flowed from his soul to hers. Their hips began to move in perfect rhythm, languorous, exotic, friction creating heat that smoldered through them. Her head fell back, exposing the tender throat, the blue vein pulsing at its base.

There his lips explored, and lower, nudging aside the neck of her leotard. Like a flower, fragrant creamy satin with luscious pink bud, she waited for him, waited for the seeking tongue and the hungry mouth. Her breasts were heavy, passion-filled, and he lifted them up with his hands, then suckled deeply, trying to draw her very essence into himself.

He peeled away her leotard, stripping it in one fluid move that left her naked before him, naked and beautiful. Kneeling, he wrapped his arms around her waist and pressed his face against the soft skin of her abdomen. She tangled her hands in his hair, rocking gently, holding tight, knowing his need.

He breathed deeply, as if by doing so he could absorb her. His hands began to move, across the swell of her hips, down her thighs, over her calves, around the delicate ankles. He bent down and kissed the arch of her right foot, then lifted it slowly and anchored her leg over his shoulder.

His hand found her, and then his tongue. Sleek, swollen, wet. He devoured her slowly while she swayed above him, rich and ripe and full of passion song.

The unsettling events of the day slipped away, and there was nothing except the delicious sensuality of the woman whose body bloomed at his touch. Time had no meaning. Place ceased to exist. It was not Kathleen who was blind, but he, blind to everything except her soft, fragrant flesh and the fires she kindled.

Hard shudders shook her once, twice, and then again. Still she had not spoken. The moment was too fragile for speech. Both of them understood that.

He slipped out of his clothes and she lay upon the floor, throwing her arms over her head and arching her back, silently offering herself to him. Poised above her, he licked the moisture from her bottom lip. She trembled, waiting. He swept his tongue across her lips again. And again. Her eyes were wide, her breath warm against his cheek.

In one fluid thrust he gave up the exquisite agony of waiting. She arched higher, her pleasure cry breaking the silence. Tremors overtook her, and he waited, buried deep, while she fell over the edge once more.

Then he began the long silken slide toward home. Slowly, softly he traveled the familiar pathway, savoring each moment of the journey. Tension built in him, pushing him faster, harder.

Sweat slicked their bodies, dampened their hair. Still they raced together through the night, panting, desperate, unable and unwilling to stop.

Lying upon her, surrounded by her sweet hot flesh, he was made whole again. And he knew that as long as he stayed in that place, in that woman, he would be complete.

Her fresh climax shook them both, and still he swept over her and through her, again and again, insatiable, invincible. Her skin had the glow of alabaster. The incandescent lights in the studio caught in the perspiration and made a shining path from her throat to her thighs. She made a small strangled cry of protest when he eased out of her. But raised on his elbows, he soothed her with his lips and tongue, tracing the shining pathway downward, pausing to delve deeply into her honeyed sweetness. With soft animal cries she clutched his shoulders and ground her hips upward, her body language telling him more clearly than words that she was as desperate as he to hold on to the moment, to stay in that magical realm.

Something dark and forbidding dwelt just beyond the boundaries of the world they'd created, and the only way they could keep it at bay was to love.

He pressed into her once more, their bodies melding as one, their limbs spread at impossible angles and tangled so that it was useless to guess where he left off and she began. Still they had not spoken, did not dare to speak.

Occasionally one of them would become perfectly still, and they would lie together with her face resting on his thigh or his lips against her breast until they regained their strength. There was no thought of time, no thought of sleep, no thought of anything except the remarkable journey they'd embarked upon.

Toward morning they reached the high bright pinnacle of oblivion. Tense, rigid, they held on to each other, crying out their joy . . . and their sorrow; for now it had come to an end. Softly they began to fall. Slowly they eased back, their sleek bodies relaxing, their breathing ragged and labored, until they lay together, a boneless heap.

Pale pink light fell upon the windowpanes and birds stirred from their perches in the branches of parasol trees that surrounded the studio. Morning had come unawares.

Hunter closed his eyes, trying to bring back the night. Feeling his pain, Kathleen brushed her lips across his face. Wordlessly he cupped her face and held it close.

"The night should never have ended," he whispered.

"I wish it hadn't."

Agony twisted his soul.

"Don't say any more, Kat."

"I must, Hunter." She ran her hands over his chest, curling her fingers into the crisp hair. "I must," she whispered.

He pulled her fiercely to him and kissed her.

"Don't, Hunter. Oh, please don't. I'm weak when you touch me."

"No. You are strong. I'm your strength and you are mine." He kissed the soft skin behind her ears, the fine sweep of her dark eyebrows, her damp cheeks, her lover-bruised lips. "Two against the world, Kat."

For a while she leaned into him, savoring his kiss, encouraging his tongue. Tension built in her once more, and he felt the tight, hard peaking of her nipples against his chest and the exquisite agony of his own arousal.

She trembled above him, and the velvet tip of his sex touched her where she was hot and moist and swollen. He waited, breathless, for the sweet slide that would catapult them once more into their own private world.

"No!" Her cry was harsh as she pushed herself away from him. Wrapping her arms tightly around her legs and pressing her face against her knees, she sat with her back to him. "I can't keep doing this."

"Doing what, my love?" Even as he asked the question he knew. Her thought processes had never been a secret to him. He knew her mind as well as he knew his own.

"Running away. Hiding."

"We're not hiding. We spent the night in your studio making love. Soon we'll shower and dress and eat breakfast and go about our usual business."

She didn't answer. Quietly he gathered their clothes. She took hers without a word. He dressed silently, watching her. In one fluid move she stood and slid into her leotard; then she shook back her hair and faced him. Her notion of where he stood was slightly off, so he moved into her line of vision. He couldn't bear the thought of Kathleen talking to the window beyond his head.

"What *is* your usual business, Hunter?"

"Diamonds."

"I know. But what do you do every day? Where do you go?"

"Sometimes to the mines. Sometimes to my office. It depends."

"You haven't been to the mines since I came, and rarely to the office. You've been baby-sitting me."

"My operation runs smoothly wherever I am and whatever I am doing."

He knew where the questions were leading, and he wanted to cover his ears like a child to shut them out.

"And where were you yesterday?"

"A small matter needed my attention." He hardly knew himself what had happened yesterday, why he had gone and what the consequences would be. If fate were kind, the matter was over and done with. She need never know, never worry.

She stared long and hard at him, seeing not with her eyes but her soul. Suddenly she balled her hands into fists and turned away.

"Kathleen?" He put his hand on her shoulder.

"I can't see your face, Hunter. I wish I could see your face."

"I'm telling you the truth. There was a small matter that needed my attention and now it's over and done with. Finished." He squeezed her shoulder, then bent and kissed the nape of her neck. "Come, my love. Let me take you back to the house."

His rich voice beguiled her; his body heat drew her to him like a moth to flame. She found herself swaying, both from fatigue and from uncertainty. Was she doing the right thing? Was she sacrificing one dream for another?

She drew apart from him, knowing that as long as he touched her, she would be under his spell.

"I'm leaving you, Hunter," she whispered. He reached for her, his hand skimming her arm. "No, please. Don't touch me. I can't do this if you touch me."

"I won't let you go."

"You have no choice."

All at once she was overcome with fatigue. She sank into the middle of the floor and covered her face with her hands.

"Kat?" He knelt beside her. "Darling, are you all right?"

"Yes. I'm fine."

The darkness. The never-ending darkness. Somehow it gave her strength.

She stood up. "Yesterday, when I woke up and found you gone, I panicked."

"I'm sorry. I should have told you I was leaving."

"No. It wasn't finding myself alone that made me afraid. It was finding myself *dependent* that scared me."

She could feel his pain building until it was a living, pulsing being, howling around the studio like a crazed animal. She wrapped her arms around herself to stop shivering.

Hunter would not easily let her go. His silence was not acquiescence but a dark brooding thunderstorm waiting to happen.

"I wanted you there with me, Hunter, acting as a buffer between me and the rest of the world. I thought how easy you made my life, how wonderful. I thought about selling my own houses and staying forever in this sweet prison with you at my side. I even thought about giving up all thoughts of returning to the stage."

"Everybody is entitled to an occasional moment of weakness."

"It wasn't an occasional *moment*, Hunter. It lasted all day."

"I shouldn't have stayed away so long."

"See. That's just what I'm talking about. All day long I listened for your footsteps, for the sound of your voice. Every few minutes I checked my watch. I didn't want to be dancing. I didn't want to be planning a comeback. I wanted nothing except to be in your arms."

He caught her shoulders and, in spite of her protests, pulled her fiercely into his embrace.

"You don't have to sacrifice anything, Kat. We'll leave together. We'll go wherever you want to go. Paris. Rome. London. New York. Just name it and we'll go there. I can conduct my business from anywhere in the world."

Heaven help her, she wanted him again, wanted to pull him onto the floor and open herself up to him. He knew. The very air became electrified with their passion.

"You can be as independent as hell, Kat. We'll live in your house with your servants and your bodyguards. We'll work everything around your schedule."

His voice was low, urgent, persuasive.

"Everything will work out," he said. "Trust me, my love." His hips moved in sweet seduction against hers. "Trust me," he whispered.

Moaning, she arched her back, grinding against him. He slid his mouth down the side of her throat, then lower.

She was gone. Lost.

She summoned her last ounce of courage and wrenched herself free.

"Trust? You call this trust? You're using my weakness against me."

"If it's weakness, then it's mine too."

One last searing touch. His hands on her hips, hers in his hair. One last lingering kiss. Mouths clinging, hearts beating hard and wild. Never wanting to let go. Never.

He drew apart slowly, then tucked her hand into the crook of his elbow. "Come, Kat. Let's go back to the house. We'll talk about this later after you've had some food and rest."

"Don't treat me like a child, Hunter." She drew her hand away.

"I'm not treating you like a child. I'm using common sense. We've been up all night. We're both tired and hungry. It's foolish to make decisions under those conditions."

"This is not a spur-of-the-moment decision, Hunter. I've known for a long time that I have to prove myself . . . alone."

"Let me help you, Kat. Don't shut me out."

All the loneliness and anxiety of the previous

day came back to her. And with it the courage to withstand the persuasive powers of Hunter La Farge.

"Isn't that what you did yesterday, Hunter? Shut me out?" His silence damned him. "You talk about trust. . . . It works both ways. If you don't trust me, how can I trust you?"

"I trust you completely," he said.

It was her turn to be silent. His long, secret absence was really no mystery to her. Sometime after dark, hours before his midnight return, she'd figured out where he was.

"What was he like, Hunter? What did you feel?"

He prowled the room like a stalking lion. She waited. At last he stood before her, filled with silent agony that brought tears to her eyes.

"Rejected," he said. "My father made me feel rejected all over again."

"I'm sorry," she whispered, reaching for him. "I'm so sorry."

He laid his cheek against her hair.

"Sweet Kathleen. You were always sweet . . . even when you were being a devil."

He stepped back, chuckling. It was a masterpiece of deceit. Hunter was trying to protect her, just as he always had, just as he always would, she supposed.

She reached for him once more and laid her hand softly against his cheek.

"Marry me, Kat," he said.

"If I marry you now, before I've proved that I can perform in public again, I may never find myself. I may be lost forever in this darkness, depending on you to lead the way."

In the hushed stillness she imagined how he looked, his dark eyes burning with intensity, his jaw strong and square, his shoulders back, his head up as he considered everything she'd said. The years spun backward, and through that tunnel of time she saw him running toward her on the school grounds, fists doubled, eyes stormy, ready to fight for her.

"How did you get that skinned knee?"

"Jamie Puckett pushed me down at recess."

"Wait right here, Kat. I'm going to find him and beat the living hell out of him."

"Then he'll just wait until you're not around and push me down again."

"Then I'll beat him up again."

"You don't have to, 'cause I'm going to beat him up myself."

That long silence she was used to while Hunter was thinking.

"Then I'll teach you how."

That was when Hunter taught her to fight like a boy.

"Please understand, Hunter," she said now as she waited.

And Hunter, who had been her best friend long before he was ever her lover, understood. He took her hand and squeezed it tight.

"Do you still remember how to fight like a boy, Kat?"

Her chin came up. "I do."

"Then get out there and knock 'em dead, kid."

"That's exactly what I intend to do."

She slid her hand into the crook of his elbow, and they walked across the compound to his house. After they'd showered and changed, they had breakfast in the courtyard, with the birds singing sweet morning melodies.

"I'm coming back to you, Hunter. In a few months, after I've proved myself, I'll be back."

"I know you will, my love. I'm sitting here trying to figure out how I'll endure all those lonely days."

"Not with another woman!"

"No. Never with another woman." He chuckled at her spunk. "Besides, I think you wore me out last night. I may never recover."

"If I weren't leaving you, I'd rise to a challenge like that."

"I was hoping you would."

"Better luck next time."

He caught her hand and pressed it to his lips.

"Next time can't come soon enough for me."

"I'll count the days," she whispered.

Two hours later she was gone.

He stood at the gates watching the dust from the Jeep swirl in the wind. He had wanted to drive her, but she'd insisted on being independent. With Martha in the driver's seat and Jake in the back, Kathleen headed proudly down the road to independence.

She'd hooted at the idea of sending bodyguards with her.

"Don't be ridiculous, Hunter. You're the diamond tycoon, not I. What can be safer than a scrawny-looking boy with his dog and his old aunt?"

"Who are you calling old?" Martha rammed her straw hat down on her head. "Old aunt, my foot. Just give me half a chance, and I'm going to leave you and that dog and go out and find myself a dancing man."

They had finally compromised: the bodyguards would accompany them to their hotel.

Spirits had been high, but it was all a sham. He'd felt the tension when he held Kathleen close for one last embrace. He'd seen it in Martha's worried face. Even the dog was not immune. Jake had been restless, tending to growl at the least disturbance.

"One last kiss," Kat had whispered as he stood at the side of the Jeep. ". . . until I come again."

Until I come again.

A cold hand closed over Hunter's heart.

Those were his words, written in a letter nearly fourteen years before and stuck in the knothole of the tree where they'd first made love. The hand squeezed his heart until he felt as if he were dying.

Would dance steal her away as Africa had stolen him?

The departing Jeep kicked up one last puff of dust, then disappeared around the bend. Hunter had to grip the iron bars of the gate to keep from running after it.

Tonight. He'd wait until later, and then he'd go after her.

"I thought I'd drop by to see if there's anything you need before you leave," he would say.

She might laugh at him and shoo Martha out the door, then pull him down onto her bed and realize that she was being stubborn after all, that she didn't have to leave him in order to make a comeback.

On the other hand, she might be furious at his lack of trust. He might risk losing her permanently.

She and Martha would be perfectly safe in the hotel in Johannesburg. And the following day she'd be on a plane leaving Africa. She hadn't said where she was going, whether it was back to her cottage in Jefferson Parish or to one of her houses or to an entirely different location.

He'd have to trust her. That was all.

Firmly he shut the gate, then strode toward

his office and called Rick the minute he was
through the door.

"I'm going to leave you in charge for a
while, Rick."

"Where are you going?"

"Somewhere where I won't think of Kathleen."

THIRTEEN

"You should come in to bed, Kathleen. The plane leaves early in the morning."

"In a little while, Martha."

Soft breezes blew against her face, bringing with them the fragrance of exotic flowers and the sound of nocturnal birds. Kathleen leaned against the balcony railing and inhaled deeply. She couldn't bear to sleep away her last few hours in Africa. In her emotionally charged state, it seemed to her that as long as she could hear the sounds and smell the fragrances that were unique to the dark continent, she would be close to Hunter.

"You and Jake go inside and get your beauty sleep. I'll be right there."

"I'll go in, but I don't like it. I promised Hunter I'd take care of you."

"You've already fulfilled that promise. You

drove like a snail coming to the hotel. Tomorrow we're going to start anew. We're going to race to the airport like carefree sports setting out on a wonderful holiday."

Martha laughed, which was exactly what Kathleen had intended. As the French doors closed behind her Kathleen wrapped her arms around herself to stop the shivers.

Something was wrong. She could feel it.

The sense of foreboding pressed at her until she had to catch the railing to keep from swooning.

"Just fatigue," she whispered, but in her heart she knew better.

If you leave, you'll never see him again.

The thought came unbidden, borne to her on the night breezes. She sank to her knees and pressed her face against the cool wrought iron. Was she buying her independence at too high a price? Suddenly all the lonely years without Hunter came back to her, the desperate longing, the secret reading of his letters, the emptiness.

"What am I doing here?" she whispered.

Hunter needed her and she needed him. She had let her own fierce pride tear them apart.

In the dark there was the soft whirring of wings as a night bird lifted toward the stars. Somewhere a tomcat called out for his mate. Sounds of late-night traffic drifted up from the streets below.

She didn't know how long she stayed where

she was with the cool railings against her skin. Hunter filled her, body and soul. It was almost as if he were there beside her, calling her name.

"I'm coming," she whispered.

The sense of urgency was so strong that she would have gone to him then if it hadn't meant waking Martha.

Tomorrow would have to be soon enough.

"Hang on, my love. . . ."

He waited in the dark.

The old woman and the dog would be out for a while. He'd used powerful tranquilizers.

He glanced toward the balcony. The woman knelt there like some fanatical moon worshiper. What in the hell was taking her so long?

Suddenly the French doors opened and she came into the room. He shrank against the wall and watched her grope her way to the bathroom. Midway there she stopped.

"Is anyone here?" she said.

He hadn't made a sound. What was she? Clairvoyant?

He squinted, trying to see in the pale moonlight that filtered through the French doors. The woman started up again, her foot barely missing the dog stretched out by the armchair.

He held his breath. It was important that she not scream. He'd caught the others unaware. After he got the dog, the fat old lady had been no problem at all. When he stuck the needle in her, she'd rolled over on her back like a hippopotamus wallowing in the mud.

The dog hadn't gone down as easily as he thought. He should have used a stronger dose. That mistake could have been fatal.

The bathroom door closed behind her and he heard the sound of running water. She might be in there awhile. Women were like that.

He settled back to wait. He had all night.

Kathleen was calling his name.

Hunter jerked awake expecting to see her standing beside his bed with her dark hair tumbled about her shoulders. Instead he saw the eternal blackness of the jungle and the glow of his campfire.

The sound of her voice whispered through him once more, and he saw her, standing on the other side of the campfire wearing white.

"Kathleen?"

Impossible. He closed his eyes and rubbed his temple. When he looked, the vision had disappeared. In his need, he'd conjured her up, just as he had that first night in Jefferson Parish.

An overwhelming sense of loss crept over him, and with it a nameless fear.

He started to pack up camp, get in his plane and go straight home. He was halfway out of his sleeping bag before reason restored itself. His overprotective instincts were what had gotten him in trouble in the first place.

He had to learn to give Kathleen the independence she needed. He settled back into his sleeping bag. There was nothing to do but wait.

There was a muffled sound, a heavy footstep falling on thick carpet, and the sense of an overpowering presence. Awakened from a sound and dreamless sleep, Kathleen lay perfectly still, listening.

"Martha?" she said softly.

The silence was dark, brooding, oppressive. Suddenly Kathleen knew she was not alone. Someone was in the room with her, someone who smelled of stale liquor and rank clothing . . . someone who would never have gotten past the door if Jake were all right.

It would be useless to call for her dog. Kathleen tried to control her terror.

And what of Martha? Was she sleeping or had the intruder done something with her?

Kathleen's terror turned to rage. Did they think she was helpless because she was blind?

After they had checked in, Martha had taken her on a guided tour of the room. If she remembered correctly, the phone was on a table beside the windows. It would be useless to her.

She eased her hand toward the bedside table. Her fingers touched the base of the lamp. One good jerk should pull the plug loose from the wall.

She closed her hand around it and waited.

The smells became stronger as the intruder closed in. Her muscles tightened in readiness. Her weapon wasn't much and she wasn't strong, but she wouldn't go down without a fight.

He was close now, so close she could hear his breathing. How close would that be? Close enough to swing the lamp and hit her target?

She tried to focus all her senses. Did he have a gun? A knife? Should she scream first and then swing? If she screamed now, would anyone come? Would he kill her?

The smell of stale liquor almost overpowered her. Biting her lip to stop herself from trembling, she tightened her grip on the lamp.

Her mind was filled with silent screams. *Hunter. Hunter.*

Rick found Martha huddled in a chair in the hotel room crying. When she saw him, she burst into a fresh gale of weeping.

The dog was stretched on the carpet at her feet.

"She's gone," Martha wailed.

"What happened?"

He tried to remain calm and seem very much in charge. The truth of the matter was that he was quaking in his boots. Broken glass was scattered on the carpet, and the lamp lay beside the bed with its base dented and its shade smashed.

"I don't know," Martha said. "When I came out of the bathroom to go to bed, she was on the balcony and Jake was on the floor. Poor Jake." She swabbed her dripping eyes and nose and tried to regain her composure.

"He's breathing." He knelt and inspected the dog. "He's heavily tranquilized, but he'll be all right. . . . You've called the police?"

"Yes." Martha surveyed the wreckage of the room, then pressed her soggy handkerchief to her mouth as the hysteria threatened once more. "What are we going to do?"

"The first thing I'm going to do is put a team of private investigators onto the case. The next thing I'll do is try to find Hunter."

Being careful to touch nothing, he walked to the bed. There was blood on the sheets.

"Hunter will kill the man who did this to her."

FOURTEEN

Johnathan was scared. The woman lay stretched out on the rude cot in the corner of the small hovel he sometimes used when he didn't want to be found. Kathleen Shaw, her identification said. The world-famous prima ballerina. The woman everybody had thought was dead.

"You've gone and done it now," he muttered.

In the light of day, his plan to bring Hunter around by capturing his woman seemed ill-conceived and foolhardy. For thirty-something years he had escaped a bum rap for murder only to blunder into a kidnapping so sensational, it would make headlines around the globe.

Sweating like a pig in the slaughterhouse, he put his hand on the woman's throat and felt for her pulse. It was weak and thready.

Groaning, he held his own head. It hurt like

hell. She'd landed him quite a blow with the lamp.

If only she hadn't fought so hard. He glared at her as if the whole situation were entirely her fault.

"Wake up, damn you."

He gave her one last accusing look, then stomped across the plank floor to his stash of liquor. When in doubt, get drunk. That was his motto.

He uncapped the bottle and took a long swig. Then holding it close to his chest, he slumped into the corner of the room so he could keep an eye on his prisoner.

Maybe he ought to tie her up. Not that she was going anywhere, and her blind as a betsy bug.

Now that he had her, what in the hell was he going to do with her?

He upended the bottle once more and drank until the liquor ran down his chin and into his collar. Then he closed his eyes and leaned his head against the wall.

His life would have been different if only he and Janice hadn't gone to the bar that night. If only that man hadn't attacked her. If only . . .

He felt a lump of self-pity rising in his throat and knew that soon he'd be soggy with whiskey and tears. Before he reached that wretched state of oblivion, he conjured up a vision of Janice.

"You're well rid of me, my darling," he whispered.

Most of the wildlife in the Serengeti had taken cover from the torrential rain, but one old leopard refused to leave his kill. Hunkered down over the baby waterbuck, he defied both rain and other animals to deprive him of his hard-earned dinner.

Hunter crouched in the bushes, his cameras slung over his shoulder. It was raining too hard for good photographs. In any case, his purpose for being in Tanzania was not photography but forgetfulness. Even as he watched the rare sight, standing close enough to see the blood on the leopard's jaws, he was achingly aware of Kathleen . . . and of his loss.

He lost track of time as he stood in the rain, and only when the leopard finished his meal did Hunter leave. He didn't see Rick until he was a few feet from his campsite. Sitting on a camp-stool in the rain, he was a forlorn sight, with his clothes soaked and the brim of his hat hanging limply around his ears.

"Rick . . . what brings you here?"

"Thank God you've come."

Hunter's heart froze. As the hard rain bit into their skin and drummed against the tent, the two friends stood facing each other, one silent with fear, the other silent with grief.

Hunter was the first to move.

"Let's go inside."

They ducked into the tent. Hunter unslung his cameras and set about making a cup of coffee.

Not Kathleen, his mind screamed.

"Trouble at the mines?" He handed Rick the steaming mug, then sat cross-legged on a colorful woven blanket, nursing his own coffee between his chilled hands.

"No. Everything is fine at the mines and at the headquarters." Rick took a long drink from his mug. His hands shook. "I've been trying to find you for two weeks."

Two weeks. Just one day short of his entire stay in the Serengeti. And not a day of it free from visions of Kathleen, dressed in white, standing beside his fire and calling his name.

"It's Kathleen," Rick said.

Hunter held up his hand as if he were warding off a blow. Silent screams were trapped in his throat.

"What has happened to Kathleen?"

"She's gone."

"Gone?" Hunter didn't know it was possible for dead men to speak, but he was speaking, moving, breathing.

"Somebody kidnapped her from the hotel room in Johannesburg."

"Martha and Jake?"

"Drugged. Kathleen was the only one taken."

"What's being done to find her?"

"A search is being conducted through official channels, of course. And I've hired a team of private investigators."

Rick's shoulders slumped as he gazed down at his cup.

"And?"

"So far they've found nothing. Not a trace."

Hunter didn't have to be told in order to understand the grave consequences. Each day that passed lessened the chances of finding her.

"Let's go," he said.

"Can we fly in this rain?"

"I'll fly through hell if I have to."

Without another word, they began to break camp. Hunter held back his rage. He would save it for the man who had taken Kathleen.

Kathleen woke up to the sound of crying. She lay in the darkness listening. The sound was harsh and guttural. Made by a man, she guessed.

She lay perfectly still, trying to learn as much as she could. There were no traffic sounds, no animal sounds, only the sound of wind and the sound of weeping.

Somebody had covered her with a light blanket. The wool scratched against her chin. Her feet were not bound, nor her hands. With great stealth she moved them under the covers. The mattress was thin and lumpy. The wall beside her bed was cool and smooth.

Was it night or day? How long had it been since her kidnapping?

She remembered the hotel room, the scuffle, the feel of the lamp breaking against the intruder's body. She thought she'd hit his head. She was proud of her aim.

The weeping stopped, and the man blew his nose. There was the sound of uneven footsteps, then glass breaking against metal.

Terror seized her as she waited. What would he do now that she was awake?

She closed her eyes quickly and tried to get her breathing back to normal. Being in a state of drugged sleep seemed safer than being awake.

The footsteps came closer, and the smell of liquor almost overwhelmed her.

"Shtill shleeping?" A finger poked her ribs. "Wake up, dammit."

Was he the only one? She listened for other footsteps, other voices.

The man standing beside her bed lifted her arm and pressed his fingers into her wrists.

"Pulsh shtill going."

He let her wrist drop, and Kathleen tried to let her arm fall naturally. The man was obviously very drunk. And alone, judging from what she could hear.

What would her chances be if she ran? Then

what? A blind woman lost in the wilds of Africa
. . . Unthinkable. She'd have to take her
chances with her captor.

Her decision made, she took a deep breath,
then threw back her covers and sat up.

"Who are you?" Her voice sounded
stronger and more authoritative than she felt.

The man made a squawking sound, and
there was a thump as he fell against the floor.
She pressed her advantage.

"How dare you take me by force." She
wanted to ask where she was, but she didn't
want to give herself away. Perhaps he didn't
know she was blind. "Are you going to answer
me, or are you going to sit there like a sniveling
coward?"

The man sniffled, but there was no movement. He was probably in no condition to get
off the floor.

"Wish I could give you back. Ish too late
. . . too late."

He sounded as mournful as the raven in
Poe's famous poem.

"Nonsense. It's never too late." Kathleen
felt dizzy. She gripped the edges of the bed to
keep from passing out. How long since she had
eaten? She remembered a blow to the side of
her head. Maybe she had a concussion.

"Get me a drink and some food and we'll
talk about how we can rectify this unfortunate
situation. I won't even demand restitution."

"Ish not you that worries me. . . . Ish Hunter."

Every nerve in her body went numb. Hysteria bubbled in her throat, and she fought it down.

"Hunter?" Her voice shook, but maybe he was too drunk to notice. "Who is Hunter?"

There was the sound of sniffling again, and then the slow rhythm of footsteps against a wooden floor. Something squeaked, a door or a drawer perhaps, being drawn open. Glassware rattled and liquid splashed against its sides.

She smelled the liquor before he pressed the cup into her hand.

"Who is Hunter?" he asked. The walk across the floor seemed to have sobered him. That or the gravity of the question. "Hunter is my son."

Anguish almost bent her double . . . anguish not for herself but for Hunter. How would he ever survive his father's final betrayal?

"Please," she said. "We have to go back. For your sake as well as for his."

Hunter's father didn't move, didn't speak. In the long dreadful silence, all she heard was the harsh sound of his breathing. Like a race car out of control, her mind careened in all different directions. Would he kill her? Why couldn't she remember the opening segment of the *Nutcracker Suite* ballet? If only she could hear the music. Would she ever smell gardenias blooming against the fence in Jefferson Parish again? Was the sun shining? She didn't want to die on a rainy day. There had been too much water on the day of Earl's death.

She tried to bring her mind under control. What were the statistics on heredity versus environment? Surely there was something of Hunter's noble nature in his father. She would appeal to that nature.

"Hunter searched for you for years. He desperately wanted a father." There was nothing but darkness and silence. She took a deep breath and tried again. "He was hurting terribly the day he came to see you. He was once again the little boy whose father rejected him."

Could she risk reaching out for him? If he had a soul, he was hurting as much as Hunter. If her aim was off, he would certainly know that she couldn't see, and that would make her twice as vulnerable.

She had to take the risk. For Hunter's sake.

Kathleen used all her powers of concentration to *see* the man standing beside her. Her senses told her he was tall. She'd have to reach high.

Were his hands hanging at his side? Was he holding a drink in one? Which one?

"Please," she whispered, taking the chance, reaching out to him. Her hand encountered flesh, a sinewy forearm covered with thick, crisp hair. She slid her hand down and caught his.

"We can work everything out. Hunter is a wonderful man."

Growling like an animal in the jungle, he shook off her hand.

"Can't take you back . . . Hunter would kill me."

His footsteps were heavy on the wooden floor. A door creaked open, and for a moment Kathleen felt a breeze and caught a whiff of exotic flowers. Then the door slammed, the lock clicked, and she was left alone with nothing to comfort her except a drink of whiskey.

Shivering, she pressed her hand over her mouth to hold back the rising hysteria. Her survival depended upon keeping her sanity.

She raised the glass to her lips and took a sip of whiskey. It helped stop the shivering. She took another cautious sip.

She'd survived an explosion and a cold, unrelenting ocean. She had no intention of buckling under to a desperate alcoholic.

Using the bed as her point of reference, she explored the room so she could learn about her prison.

Hunter sat in the police station listening to a report on the evidence gathered from the hotel room.

"Some of the blood belonged to Kathleen Shaw," the man said. He was small, wiry, intense, and baffled. A two-week search had yielded very little.

"Some?" Hunter asked.

"Yes. The other was the same type as the man who calls himself Tokolosh."

Tokolosh. Mongo. The Black Knight. Johnathan McFarland. His father. The man who could vanish for years and never be found.

"Mr. La Farge? Do you need something . . . a cup of coffee? A drink of water?"

Hunter left his chair to stand beside the window. It was dark outside. Kathleen was always in the dark. He rammed his hands into his pockets to keep from smashing them through the wall; then he turned back to the earnest young man sitting at the desk.

"I need a miracle."

FIFTEEN

Kathleen devised her own braille calendar. Each day she used her fork to make a notch on the headboard.

She was never given a knife. Probably because Hunter's father remembered the way she'd attacked him with the lamp.

Hunter's father. She still didn't know his name. He brought her meals, if stringy unidentifiable meat and bland rice could be called a meal.

Her hope of keeping her blindness a secret was quickly dashed. When he had come back from his long absence that first day of her captivity, he had shoved food into her hands then asked her if she knew how to use a fork.

"I'm blind, not stupid."

Hatred threatened to obscure her reason. She brought it quickly under control. How could she hate the man who had fathered Hunter?

Twice a day he tied her hands with a rope and led her outside for exercise. She struggled against feeling like an animal.

"Untie me," she said the third day. "I won't run away."

"No."

"Where would I possibly go? I'm blind."

"Being blind didn't stop you from knocking a knot on my head. I don't trust you, lady."

"That makes two of us. I don't trust you."

To her surprise he laughed, then she felt the rope being pulled from her hands. It was only a small victory, but she was too smart to discount it, no matter how small.

Smoke from a strong cigar competed with the smells of exotic flowers and fertile soil.

"You've got spunk," he said.

"Thank you."

The smoke curled around her head. She waited, letting him take the lead.

"You remind me of Janice."

Hunter's mother. It was a major breakthrough. Kathleen dared to hope.

"I grew up next door to Hunter and his mother," she said.

The breath he drew was harsh. She felt the tension in him. Her own heart felt as if it would beat out of her chest.

"Would you like me to tell you about her?" she asked softly.

Her only answer was the mocking laughter of a distant hyena.

Don't push, she told herself. Wait. Listen.

When Hunter's father spoke, his voice was so soft, she had to strain to hear.

"Did she ever have another man?" he asked.

"Never."

There was a sound like wind blowing through the trees, and she realized it was Hunter's father, sighing. Kathleen touched her locket for luck and courage.

"She was totally devoted to Hunter," she said. "There was never anyone else in her life from the day he was born until the day she died."

"Enough!"

His yell was filled with pain. Instantly Kathleen understood her mistake. Hunter's father had not known that Janice was dead.

"I'm so sorry," she whispered. "Everything is going to be all right. We can *make* it be all right."

"Just shut up. I don't want your damned sympathy, and I sure as hell don't want your advice. . . ."

She waited, hoping for another break.

"Walk." His voice cut through her like a whip. "Ten feet forward and ten feet back. Don't bump into any damned trees and keep your mouth shut. I don't want to hear any female palavering."

Kathleen thrust her chin out and walked. Triumphant. She had won another small victory. Her hands were still untied, and she knew a little bit more about Hunter's father.

She counted her steps. The sweet fragrance became stronger.

"Are there flowers here?"

"Yes. Dammit. I said don't talk."

Kneeling, she searched with both hands until she encountered a waxy blossom. She snapped the delicate stem.

"Damned stubborn female," he said.

Kathleen smiled. She *was* stubborn. But more than that, she was strong, even in captivity. As she tucked the flower behind her ear she understood that she'd always been strong, that she'd never had to leave to Hunter. The courage she had thought she got from him had been inside her all along.

Kathleen felt a vaulting sense of freedom, even when Hunter's father led her back inside and locked the door.

Though it was still summer and hot outside, Hunter built a fire to take the chill out of his bones. Still in his flight gear, he sank into a chair and stretched his hands out to the flame.

He had been searching for days. . . . Five? Six? He'd lost count.

The door opened quietly and Martha and Rick slipped inside. She had aged since the beginning of the ordeal, and Rick had lost weight.

"Any news?" Rick asked.

"Nothing," Hunter said, trying to keep the fear out of his voice.

"They can't just drop off the face of the earth," Martha said.

"Tokolosh is an expert at vanishing," Rick told her, his eyes as bleak as winter. "But Hunter will soon find him."

"Sure he will." Martha's cheerful voice rang false.

"Damned right," Rick said.

They were talking to each other as if Hunter were not even there. He knew they meant well, but he couldn't stand the hopelessness on their faces.

"I'd like to rest now," he said. "It's been a long week."

They left quietly, closing the door behind them. The fire crackled in the grate, and in the flames he could see the vast expanses of Africa, beautiful and treacherous . . . and empty of Kathleen.

"Damn you, Johnathan McFarland. Damn you to hell."

The fire hissed and slowly its warmth spread

through his body. Weary, Hunter closed his eyes.

She came to him in a whisper of silk, her white dress molded against her legs and her gold necklace burning bright as a flame against her lily skin.

"The music's playing," she whispered. *"Dance with me."*

Her hair was soft, her lips sweet. When he touched her, the white dress dissolved and she was naked in arms. Sleek. Silky. Hot. He fell into her, groaning.

"I thought I'd lost you," he said.

"Never."

She twisted beneath him, burning, melting. He held fast.

"Stay," he whispered. *But he couldn't keep her. She dissolved in his arms and he was left clutching nothing but air.*

Hunter jerked awake. He felt like a traitor, sleeping while Kathleen was . . . He couldn't bear to think what might be happening to her.

"Hunter."

Her voice was as soft as the breezes that stirred the parasol trees outside the French doors. He pressed his hands against his tired eyes. The vision was haunting him now, even when he was awake.

"Hunter." Her hand lay upon his shoulder, the blue veins stark against her white skin.

His heart slammed so hard against his chest,

he could hardly breathe. He swiveled slowly and there she was, standing beside his chair as fragile as a gardenia, thin and pale but alive. God, she was alive!

"Kathleen . . . Kathleen."

She knelt beside his chair, and he caught her face between his hands.

"If you're a dream, I don't want to wake up," he said.

"I'm not a dream." She turned her face against his palms and kissed them. "I'm real."

While flames cast shadows against the wall they absorbed each other. His hands trembled on her cheeks, and the tears that fell against them melted and became a part of his soul.

There were so many things he had to ask her. Where she had been. How she had been treated. How she got home. But all that could wait. She was safe now, and he would keep her that way.

"Don't ever leave me again," he whispered.

"Never." She kissed his palm, the inside of his wrist, then pressed his hand against the gold locket that rested between her breasts. "Never, my love."

His hand closed around the locket, and with his thumb he pressed the catch. Inside was the picture of the two of them, forever young, laughing, and in love.

They were no longer young, but the laughter and the love would be theirs. Forever.

He snapped the locket shut, then leaned down and tenderly brushed his lips across the tops of her breasts.

"Hunter," she whispered. "We're not alone."

He heard the sound at the door. A discreet cough. Heavy breathing.

His muscles tensed as he whirled around. Johnathan McFarland stood in the doorway, a slouch hat drawn low over his eyes and a gun slung over his shoulder.

"Don't even think about trying anything," he said. "I may be old, but this gun is loaded and I'm damned fast on the draw."

Hunter stood up and stepped away from Kathleen.

"You'd better make the first shot count, because I'm going to kill you."

"Like father, like son."

"Like hell."

"I killed for the woman I loved once. Killed to defend her honor."

With his hands held over his head, Johnathan left the doorway and stepped onto the thick carpet.

"Stay right where you are," Hunter said.

"I'm harmless. Ask Kathleen."

"Hunter, Johnathan was good to me."

"He took you by force. He's kept you God only knows where for nearly a month. Don't talk to me about how *good* he is."

"He's your father."

"I don't have a father."

Primitive rage boiled through Hunter. The man in the doorway had deprived him of the woman who was his heart, his life, his soul. Hunter felt an animalistic urge to tear him apart with his bare hands.

"Hunter . . ." Kathleen's quiet voice and her hand on his arm made him human again. "Listen to what he has to say. If not for your sake, then for mine. Please."

Johnathan stood just inside the doorway with his hands still held in the air. Nothing he said could possibly make any difference to Hunter.

"I didn't want to leave you and Janice," he said. "I *had* to."

At the mention of his mother's name, Hunter remembered the way her face had softened when she spoke of his father, remembered the dress in her closet with the dead corsage pinned to it.

"Did you ever think about coming back?" Hunter asked. "About hiring a good lawyer and trying to get justice?"

"What kind of justice would a poor, out-of-work bum have gotten?"

All the rage of his childhood weighed Hunter down, and he would give Johnathan no quarter.

"I had no name. I was a bastard, fighting for everything I had."

"Do you think a convict father would have enhanced your childhood?"

"What do you want from me? More money?"

Johnathan took a step closer. It was difficult to hold on to his rage, looking straight into his father's blue eyes.

"I feel the same obligation you felt for me," Hunter said. "None."

"I don't want your money. . . ." His father was close enough now that Hunter could see the tears. "I want your forgiveness."

Rage propelled Hunter to shout *No!* but caution held him back. For every man there was a pivotal moment that decided his destiny. In the hushed stillness of that room, with the only sound coming from the fire that crackled in the grate, Hunter understood that he had come to a crossroads.

He swiveled his head to look at Kathleen. The instant his gaze fell upon her, she knew. She reached out to him, and he took her hand.

They didn't need words. Her courage flowed through him, and his strength fortified her. He squeezed her hand once for reassurance, then turned to face his father.

"Being a part of this family doesn't come without a price," he said. "There are rules that must be obeyed."

Johnathan squared his shoulders. "I reckon a man is never too old to learn."

Kathleen's arms slid around Hunter, and he drew her close.

"The first rule is don't hover over Kathleen," he said.

Johnathan McFarland threw back his head and laughed.

"Hell, I don't need any young buck to tell me that. She'd the damnedest woman I ever met . . . besides your mother. Now, there was a woman. . . ."

Hunter reached for his father's hand and drew him into the circle beside the warm fire.

SIXTEEN

Lincoln Center was filled to capacity, and thousands lined the streets hoping for a glimpse of the world's greatest ballerina, who had come back from the dead. In three front-row center seats were one stout proud old woman and two men who had the look of fierce lions, one young, one old.

Resplendent in his tuxedo, Johnathan held his breath as the curtain opened. The stage looked like something out of a fairy tale. Hell, his whole life lately was something out of a fairy tale. It was filled with every luxury imaginable—expensive clothes, fines houses, new cars.

The thing he wanted most, though, was the love and respect of his son. He had done everything possible—given up the bottle, which turned out to be one of hardest battles he'd ever waged. He hadn't thought of himself as an alcoholic until he'd begun to fight that difficult battle. He'd mostly given up cussing, though he still liked to mix it up with Hunter's guards just to keep in practice.

When Hunter had shaved off his beard, Johnathan had taken to shaving daily, but he refused to cut off his ponytail. Judging from the predatory looks some of the women were giving him, he figured he'd made the right decision. Even Martha looked at him with a light in her eyes.

Of course the thing they didn't know was that Janice was enshrined in his heart and there would never be room for another woman.

Sometimes his life seemed like a dream to him, and he had to pinch himself to know it was all real.

The orchestra began playing, and Hunter drew in a sharp breath. Johnathan turned to look at his son. He was rigid with tension, his eyes riveted to the stage.

"She'll be all right," Johnathan whispered.

"Damned right."

Johnathan had to fight against tears when Hunter smiled at him. If it wasn't love and respect, it was close. In time, the rest would come.

"There she is," Johnathan whispered.

Kathleen Shaw La Farge, the program said, dancing excerpts from *Giselle*.

Johnathan didn't know squat about ballet, but he knew that Kathleen was the best and that she'd never danced as anything except Shaw, even when she was married to Earl Lennox.

La Farge. A fictitious name that Hunter had made worthy. A name that Kathleen would make famous on the stage.

A hush fell over the audience. Kathleen stood in the spotlight with her chin pointed upward.

Lord, could she do it? Johnathan gripped the edges of his seat. When she began to dance, he knew that he was watching magic.

She finished to thunderous applause. The audience rose to its feet, chanting her name.

"Kathleen . . . Kathleen . . . Kathleen . . ."

He turned to see how Hunter was taking the pressure, but his son was already headed backstage.

"That's my daughter-in-law, you know," he said to the woman sitting next to him.

"Really?" The woman beamed. "We saw her in Paris two years ago. She's even better now than she was then."

Not blind, but better. He'd have to remember to tell Kathleen.

"By the way, I'm Mrs. Gertrude Walton."

Suddenly he knew that there was one final act of trust he could do to make them a family; he would officially take his son's name.

"I'm Johnathan La Farge," he said. "And damned proud of it."

❖————————❖

Kathleen took her final bow. Applause and shouts of *"Brava!"* washed over her. This was the moment she'd waited for, the dream she'd worked for.

When she left the stage, the audience was still calling her name. Jake would be waiting for her in the wings to take her back to the dressing room.

"Magnificent, Kathleen."

"Perfectly beautiful performance. Flawless."

"Superb."

The backstage crew surrounded her, offering their congratulations. So many voices. So many people she couldn't see.

She reached for Jake's harness. That's when she felt his presence. Her husband. Hunter La Farge. The man she could pick out in a crowd of millions. The man who made all other dreams seem pale.

"Hunter . . ."

He stepped forward and wrapped his arms around her. His lips brushed hers.

"You are magic, Kat. Watching you, I almost forgot that you're my wife."

"I don't ever intend to let you forget that."

The backstage crowd parted to let them through. When they reached her dressing room, she stationed Jake outside the door.

"Don't let a soul in, Jake," she said. "Guard it with your life."

"Sounds ominous, Mrs. La Farge." Hunter slid her elaborately beaded costume off her shoulders. She was already ripe for him. "Should I be worried?"

"Indeed, you should." She laced her fingers through his hair and pulled him down to her breast.

Soon the waves of passion that swept over her would become a full-fledged hurricane. Soon she would be beyond speech.

"This is just the beginning," she said. "London. Rome. Paris. Jefferson Parish."

"Jefferson Parish?"

Her body screamed in protest as Hunter left off his erotic attentions.

"There's a little back room at the cottage that will make a perfect nursery," she whispered.

"You want children?"

Kathleen trembled inside. They'd never discussed children. What if Hunter didn't want them? What if the scars of his own childhood were too deep? Most horrible of all, what if he were afraid for her to be a mother because she was blind?

"Yes," she said. "When the time is right."

A great stillness descended on him, and she waited, entrusting her last dream to him. With children, her life would be perfect; but even if he said no, her world would be complete. She had ballet and she had Hunter.

"Kat . . ." He caught her hands and pressed her palms against his mouth. His lips were warm, and on them she felt his tears. "It will do me great honor to be the father of your children. I will make La Farge a name to bear with pride."

"My love . . . my dearest love . . . La Farge is already a name to bear with pride."

She pulled him down to her, and as their bodies merged, so did their hearts and souls. As always, Hunter knew what she was thinking. Before they started that long journey that would take away reason, he lifted himself on his elbows and brushed his lips against the golden locket that nestled between her breasts.

"We are one, Kat. Now and forever."

THE EDITOR'S CORNER

What an irresistible lineup we have for you next month! These terrific romances from four of our most talented authors deliver wonderful heroines and sexy heroes. They are full of passion, fun, and intensity—just what you need to keep warm on those crisp autumn nights.

Starting things off is **ONE ENCHANTED AUTUMN,** LOVESWEPT #710, from supertalented Fayrene Preston, and enchanted is exactly how Matthew Stone feels when he meets the elegant attorney Samantha Elliott. She's the one responsible for introducing his aunt to her new beau, and wary that the beau might be a fortune hunter, Matthew is determined to stop the wedding. Samantha invites Matthew to dinner, sure that seeing the loving couple together will convince the cynical reporter, but she soon finds herself the object of Matthew's own amorous pursuit. Another utterly romantic novel of unexpected passion and exquisite sensuality from Fayrene.

Billie Green is back with **STARWALKER**, LOVESWEPT #711, a unique and sexy romance that'll have you spellbound. Born of two bloods, torn between two worlds, Marcus Aurelius Reed is arrogant, untamed—and the only man who can save Laken Murphy's brother's life. She needs a Comanche shaman to banish an unseen evil, but he refuses to help her, swears the man she seeks no longer exists. Her persistence finally pays off, but the real challenge begins when Laken agrees to share his journey into a savage past. Tempted by this lord of dark secrets, Laken must now trust him with her wild heart. Once more Billie seduces her fans with this enthralling story of true love.

Victoria Leigh gives us a heroine who only wants to be **BLACKTHORNE'S WOMAN**, LOVESWEPT #712. Micah Blackthorne always captures his quarry, but Bethany Corbett will do anything to elude her pursuer and keep her baby safe—risk her life on snowy roads, even draw a gun! But once she understands that he is her only chance for survival, she pleads for a truce and struggles to prove her innocence. Micah refuses to let his desire for the beautiful young mother interfere with his job, but his instincts tell him she is all she claims to be . . . and more. In a world of betrayal and dark desire, only he can command her surrender—and only she can possess his soul. Victoria has created a thrilling tale of heated emotions, racing pulses, and seductive passions that you won't be able to put down.

Please give a big welcome to Elaine Lakso, whose debut novel will have you in **HIGH SPIRITS**,

LOVESWEPT #713. Cody McRae is tall, dark, dangerously unpredictable—and the only man Cass MacFarland has ever loved! Now, six years after he's accused her of betrayal, she is back in town . . . and needs his help to discover if her spooky house is truly haunted. As wickedly handsome as ever, Cody bets Cass he is immune to her charms—but taking his dare might mean getting burned by the flames in his eyes. Funny, outrageous, and shamelessly sexy, this wonderful novel offers spicy suspense and two unforgettable characters whose every encounter strikes romantic sparks.

Happy reading!

With warmest wishes,

Beth de Guzman

Beth de Guzman

Senior Editor

P.S. Don't miss the women's novels coming your way in October. In the blockbuster tradition of Julie Garwood, **THIEF OF HEARTS** by Teresa Medeiros is a captivating historical romance of adventure and triumph; **VIRGIN BRIDE** by Tamara Leigh is an electrifying medieval romance in which a woman falls in love with her mortal enemy; **COURTING MISS HATTIE** by award-winning author Pamela Morsi is an unforgettable novel in which handsome Reed Tylor shares a scorching kiss with Hattie Colfax and realizes that his best friend is the only woman he will ever love. We'll be giving you a sneak peek at these wonderful books in next month's LOVESWEPTs. And immediately following this page, look for a preview of the terrific romances from Bantam that are *available now!*

"One of the genre's most creative writers. Her ingenious romances always entertain and leave readers with a warm glow."
—*Romantic Times*

Betina Krahn

THE LAST BACHELOR

Betina Krahn, author of the national bestsellers THE PRINCESS AND THE BARBARIAN and MY WARRIOR'S HEART, is one of the premier names in romance. Now, with this spectacularly entertaining battle of the sexes, her distinctive humor and charm shine brighter than ever.

Antonia's bedroom was a masterpiece of Louis XIV opulence . . . in shades of teal and seafoam and ecru, with touches of gilt, burnt umber, and apricot. Sir Geoffrey had spared no expense to see to her pleasure and her comfort: from the hand-tinted friezes on the ceilings, to the ornate floor-to-ceiling bed, to the thick Aubusson carpets, to the exquisite tile stove, hand-painted with spring flowers, he had imported from Sweden to insure the room would be evenly warm all winter. Every shape, every texture was lush and feminine, meant to delight her eye and satisfy her touch . . . the way her youth and beauty and energy had delighted her aging husband. It was her personal retreat, a balm for her spirits, her sanctuary away from the world.

And Remington Carr had invaded it.

When she arrived breathless at her chamber door, she could see that the heavy brocades at the windows had been gathered back and the south-facing windows had been thrown open to catch the sultry breeze. Her hand-painted and gilded bed was mounded with bare ticking, and her linens, comforters, and counterpane were piled in heaps on the floor around the foot of the bed. It took a moment to locate Remington.

He stood by her dressing table with his back to her, his shirt sleeves rolled up and his vest, cravat, and collar missing. The sight of his long, black-clad legs and his wide, wedge-shaped back sent a distracting shiver through her. When his head bent and his shoulder flexed, she leaned to one side to see what he was doing.

He was holding one of her short black gloves and as she watched, he brought it to his nose, closed his eyes, and breathed in. A moment later, he strolled to the nearby bench, where her shot-silk petticoat and French-cut corset—the purple satin one, covered with black Cluny lace—lay exactly as she had left them the evening before. She looked on, horrified, as he lifted and wiggled the frilly hem of her petticoat, watching the delicate flounces wrap around his wrist. Abandoning that, he ran a speculative hand over the molded cups at the top of her most elegant stays, then dragged his fingers down the front of them to toy with the suspenders that held up her stockings. She could see his smile in profile.

"No garters," he murmured, just loud enough to hear in the quiet.

"Just what do you think you are doing?" she demanded, lurching forward a step before catching herself.

He turned sharply, then relaxed into a heart-stopping smile at the sight of her.

"Women's work . . . what else?" he said in insufferably pleasant tones. "I've just given your featherbeds a sound thrashing, and I am waiting for the dust to clear so I can get on with turning your mattresses."

"My mattresses don't need turning, thank you," she charged, her face reddening. "No more than my most personal belongings need plundering. How dare you invade my bedchamber and handle my things?" She was halfway across the room before she realized he wasn't retreating, and that, in fact, the gleam in his eyes intensified as she approached, making it seem that he had been waiting for her. Warnings sounded in her better sense and she halted in the middle of the thick carpet.

"Put those back"—she pointed to the gloves in his hand—"and leave at once."

He raised one eyebrow, then glanced at the dainty black seven-button glove he held. "Only the best Swedish kid, I see. One can always tell Swedish glove leather by the musk that blends so nicely with a woman's own scent. Your scent is roses, isn't it?" He inhaled the glove's scent again and gave her a desirous look. "I do love roses."

He was teasing, flirting with her again . . . the handsome wretch. It was no good appealing to his sense of shame; where women were concerned, he didn't seem to have one. Her only hope, she realized, was to maintain her distance and her composure and use deflating candor to put him in his place. And his place, she told her racing heart, was anywhere *except* the middle of her bedroom.

"You rush headlong from one outrage into another, don't you, your lordship?" she declared, crossing her arms and resisting the hum of excitement rising in her blood. "You haven't the slightest regard for decency or propriety—"

"I do wish you would call me Remington," he said with exaggerated sincerity. "I don't think a first-name-basis would be considered too much familiarity with a man who is about to climb into your bed and turn it upside down." Trailing that flagrant double entendre behind him, he tossed her glove aside and started for the bed.

"Into my . . . ?" Before she could protest, he was indeed climbing up into the middle of her bed, pushing the featherbed to the foot of the bed and seizing the corners of the mattress. As the ropes shifted and groaned and the thick mattress began to roll, she felt a weightless sensation in the pit of her stomach and understood that he was moving more than just a cotton-stuffed ticking. The sight of him in those vulnerable confines was turning her inside out, as well.

"Come down out of there this instant, Remington Carr!" She hurried to the edge of the bed, frantic to get him out of it.

"I have a better idea," he said, shoving to his feet and bracing his legs to remain stable on the springy ropes. "Why don't you come up here? There's plenty of room." He flicked a suggestive look around him, then pinned it on her. "You know, this is a very large bed for a woman who sleeps by herself. How long has it been, Antonia, since you've had your ticking turned?"

A romance of mystery, magic,
and forbidden passion

PRINCE OF WOLVES
by
Susan Krinard

"A brilliantly talented new author."
—*Romantic Times*

*Through with running from the past, Joelle Randall had
come to the rugged Canadian Rockies determined to face
her pain and begin anew. All she needed was a guide to
lead her through the untamed mountain wilderness to the
site where her parents' plane had crashed so long ago. But
the only guide Joelle could find was Luke Gévaudan, a
magnetically attractive loner with the feral grace of a wolf
and eyes that glittered with a savage intensity. She couldn't
know that Luke was the stuff of legends, one of the last
survivors of an ancient race of werewolves . . . a man
whose passion she would not be able to resist—no matter
how terrible the price.*

Joey was too lost in her own musings to immediately
notice the sudden hush that fell over the bar. The
absence of human chatter caught her attention slowly,
and she blinked as she looked around. The noisy
clumps of men were still at their tables, but they

seemed almost frozen in place. Only the television, nearly drowned out before, broke the quiet.

There was a man standing just inside the doorway, as still as all the others, a silhouette in the dim light. It took Joey a moment to realize that he was the focus of this strange and vivid tableau.

Even as the thought registered, someone coughed. It broke the hush like the snap of a twig in a silent forest. The room suddenly swelled again with noise, a relieved blast of sound as things returned to normal.

Joey turned to Maggie.

"What was that all about?" she asked. Maggie was slow to answer, but the moment of gravity was short-lived, and the barkeep smiled again and shook her head.

"Sorry about that. Must have seemed pretty strange, I guess. But he tends to have that effect on people around here."

Joey leaned forward on her elbow, avoiding a wet puddle on the counter. "Who's 'he'?" she demanded, casting a quick glance over her shoulder.

Setting down the mug she'd been polishing, Maggie assumed an indifference Joey was certain she didn't feel. "His name is Luke Gévaudan. He lives some way out of town—up the slope of the valley. Owns a pretty big tract of land to the east."

Joey slewed the stool around to better watch the man, chin cupped in her hand. "I know you've said people here don't much care for outsiders," she remarked, "but you have to admit that was a pretty extreme reaction. . . . Gévaudan, you said. Isn't that a French name?"

"French-Canadian," Maggie corrected.

"So he's one of these . . . French-Canadians? Is

that why the people here don't like him?" She studied Maggie over her shoulder.

"It's not like that," Maggie sighed. "It's hard to explain to someone from outside—I mean, he's strange. People don't trust him, that's all. And as a rule he doesn't make much of an attempt to change that. He keeps to himself."

Unexpectedly intrigued, Joey divided her attention between the object of her curiosity and the redhead. "Don't kid me, Maggie. He may be strange and he may be standoffish, but you can't tell me that wasn't more than just mild distrust a minute ago."

Maggie leaned against the bar and sagged there as if in defeat. "I said it's complicated. I didn't grow up here, so I don't know the whole story, but there are things about the guy that bother people. I hear he was a strange kid." She hesitated. "He's also got a bit of a reputation as a—well, a ladykiller, I guess you could say." She grinned and tossed her red curls. "I'm not sure that's the right word. Let's put it this way—he's been known to attract the ladies, and it's caused a bit of a ruckus now and then."

"Interesting," Joey mused. "If he's so popular with the local women, I can see why the men around here wouldn't be overly amused."

"It's not just local women," Maggie broke in, falling naturally into her usual habit of cozy gossip. "Though there were a couple of incidents—before my time, you understand. But I know there've been a few outsiders who've, shall we say, taken up with him." She gave an insinuating leer. "They all left, every one of them, after a few months. And none of them ever talked."

Wondering when she'd get a clear look at his face, Joey cocked an eye at her friend. "I guess that could make for some resentment. He may be mysterious, but he doesn't sound like a very nice guy to me."

"There you go," Maggie said, pushing herself off the bar. "Consider yourself warned." She winked suggestively. "The way you're staring at him, I'd say you need the warning."

At Joey's start of protest, Maggie sashayed away to serve her customers. Joey was left to muse on what she'd been told. Not that it really mattered, in any case. She wasn't interested in men. There were times when she wondered if she ever would be again. But that just wasn't an issue now. She had far more important things on her mind. . . .

Her thoughts broke off abruptly as the man called Gévaudan turned. There was the briefest hush again, almost imperceptible; if Joey hadn't been so focused on him and what had happened, she might never have noticed. For the first time she could see him clearly as he stepped into the light.

The first impression was of power. It was as if she could see some kind of aura around the man—too strong a feeling to dismiss, as much as it went against the grain. Within a moment Joey had an instinctive grasp of why this Luke Gévaudan had such a peculiar effect on the townspeople. He seemed to be having a similar effect on her.

Her eyes slid up his lithe form, from the commonplace boots and over the snug, faded jeans that molded long, muscular legs. She skipped quickly over his midtorso and took in the expanse of chest and broad shoulders, enhanced rather than hidden by the deep green plaid of his shirt. But it was when she reached his face that the full force of that first impression hit her.

He couldn't have been called handsome—not in

that yuppified modern style represented by the clean-cut models in the ads back home. There was a roughness about him, but not quite the same unpolished coarseness that typified many of the local men. Instead, there was a difference—a uniqueness—that she couldn't quite compare to anyone she'd seen before.

Her unwillingly fascinated gaze traveled over the strong, sharply cut lines of his jaw, along lips that held a hint of reserved mobility in their stillness. His nose was straight and even, the cheekbones high and hard, hollowed underneath with shadow. The hair that fell in tousled shocks over his forehead was mainly dark but liberally shot with gray, especially at the temples. The age this might have suggested was visible nowhere in his face or body, though his bearing announced experience. His stance was lightly poised, alert, almost coiled, like some wary creature from the wilds.

But it wasn't until she reached his eyes that it all coalesced into comprehension. They glowed. She shook her head, not sure what she was seeing. It wasn't a literal glow, she reminded herself with a last grasp at logic, but those eyes shone with their own inner light. They burned—they burned on hers. Her breath caught in her throat. He was staring at her, and for the first time she realized he was returning her examination.

She met his gaze unflinchingly for a long moment. His eyes were pale—and though in the dim light she could not make out the color, she could sense the warm light of amber in their depths. Striking, unusual eyes. Eyes that burned. Eyes that seemed never to blink but held hers in an unnerving, viselike grip. Eyes that seemed hauntingly familiar. . . .

Joey realized she was shaking when she finally

looked away. Her hands were clasped together in her lap, straining against each other with an internal struggle she was suddenly conscious of. Even now she could feel his gaze on her, intense and unwavering, but she resisted the urge to look up and meet it again. The loss of control she'd felt in those brief, endless moments of contact had been as unexpected and frightening as it was inexplicable. She wasn't eager to repeat the experience. But the small, stubborn core of her that demanded control over herself and her surroundings pricked at her without mercy. With a soft curse on an indrawn breath, Joey looked up.

He was gone.

Some secrets are too seductive to keep, and too dangerous to reveal.

WHISPERED LIES
by
Christy Cohen

For thirty-seven years Leah Shaperson had been trapped in a marriage devoid of passion. Then a stranger's tantalizing touch awakened her desires, and she found that she'd do anything to feel wanted once more . . . even submit to reckless games and her lover's darkest fantasies. But she would soon learn that the price of forbidden pleasure is steep. . . .

"I know," Elliot said. His voice was hoarse and the words were garbled.

"What?"

"I said I know," Elliot said, turning to her. He showed her a face she didn't recognize, red with suppressed rage. She clutched her nightgown to her chest.

"You know what?" she asked. She would make him say it. She still could not believe he knew. No one could know and not say anything. He had come home on time tonight and they'd had dinner together. How could he sit through a whole dinner with her and not say anything? How could he have sat through so many dinners, gotten through so many days, and still kept quiet?

Elliot stepped toward her, his face and neck blistering from rage, and Leah saw James's face in his. She saw the recklessness, the fury, the need to lash out. She stepped back, but then Elliot turned from her and lunged for the bed. He yanked the blankets off and threw them on the floor. Then he grabbed the pillows, flung them hard against the mattress, then hurled them across the room. He stared back at her, burned her with his gaze, then, in one viciously graceful move, swiped his arm across the dresser, knocking over frames and bottles of perfume. Glass shattered on the hardwood floor and liquid seeped into the wood, bombarding the room with fragrances.

Elliot looked around wildly. He started toward her and Leah jumped back, but then he turned and ran to the closet. He flung open the door and grabbed one of Leah's blouses. He ripped it off the hanger, then hurled it at her face.

Leah watched this man, this alien man, as he ripped off blouse after blouse and flung each one at her harder than the one before. She did not back away when the clothes hit her. She took every shot, was somehow relieved at the stinging on her cheeks, as if, after all, she was getting what she'd always thought she deserved.

She stood in silence, in awe, in dreamlike fear. Elliot went through the entire closet, ripped out every piece of her clothing. When he was through, he picked up her shoes and sailed them right for her head. Leah screamed and ducked and then, for the first time, understood that he hated her and ran out of the room.

He was faster and he grabbed her before she could get to the bathroom to lock herself inside. He pulled her into the kitchen, flipped on the glaring fluorescent lights, and fixed her with a stare that chilled her.

"I know you've been seeing James Arlington for three years," he said, the words straight and precise as arrows. "I know you've gone to him every Tuesday and Thursday night and screwed his brains out in his office. I know you went to him the day we got home from the cabin."

Leah slumped, and as if every word were a fist pounding on her head, she fell toward the floor. By the time he was through, she was down on her knees, crying. He stared at her, seemed to finally see her through his fury, and then pushed her away in disgust. She had to brace herself to keep from crashing into the kitchen cabinets.

"I've always known!" Elliot shouted. "You thought I was a fool, that I'd stopped looking at you. But I was always looking. Always!"

"So why didn't you do anything?" Leah shouted back up at him.

His eyes were wide, frenzied, and Leah pulled herself up. She backed into the corner of the kitchen.

"Because I loved you," he said, his anger turning to pain. He started crying, miming sounds with his mouth. Leah was both repulsed and drawn to him. She didn't know a thing about him, she realized in that instant. She had not known he was capable of shouting, of going crazy, of ransacking their bedroom. She had not known he could feel so much pain, that he must have been feeling it all along.

"Because," he went on when he could, "I thought it would pass. I thought you'd come back to me."

"I never left you," Leah said.

Elliot's head jerked up and his tears stopped abruptly. The knives sat on the counter by his hand and he pulled out a steak knife. Leah's eyes widened as he fingered the blade.

"You think I'm crazy," he said. "You think I'd hurt you."

"I don't know what to think."

He stepped toward her, smiling, the knife still in his hand. She raised her hand to her mouth, and then Elliot quickly turned and threw the knife across the room like a carnival performer. It landed in the sofa and stuck out like an extremity.

"I saw him open the door to you," Elliot said, grabbing her arm. "His fancy silk robe was hanging open. I could see him from the road. I kept thinking, 'She won't walk in. Leah would be sickened by a display like that.' But you weren't. You were eating it up."

"He makes me feel things!" Leah shouted. She was the one who was crying now. "He wants me. He's excited by me. You can't even—"

They stared at each other and, for a moment, Elliot came back to her. His face crumbled, the anger disintegrated, and she saw him, her husband. She touched his cheek.

"Oh, El, we've got to stop this."

He jerked away at her touch and stood up straight. He turned around and walked back to the bedroom. He looked at the mess in confusion, as if he couldn't remember what he had done. Then he walked to the closet, pulled out the suitcase, and opened it up on the bed.

Leah came in and stood by the door. She thought, *I'm dreaming. If anyone's going to leave, it will be me.* But as she thought this, Elliot packed his underwear and socks and shirts and pants in his suitcase and then snapped it shut.

He walked past her without a word. He set the suitcase down by the front door and then walked into the dining room. He took his briefcase off the table and walked out the door.

OFFICIAL RULES

To enter the sweepstakes below carefully follow all instructions found elsewhere in this offer.

The **Winners Classic** will award prizes with the following approximate maximum values: 1 Grand Prize: $26,500 (or $25,000 cash alternate); 1 First Prize: $3,000; 5 Second Prizes: $400 each; 35 Third Prizes: $100 each; 1,000 Fourth Prizes: $7.50 each. Total maximum retail value of Winners Classic Sweepstakes is $42,500. Some presentations of this sweepstakes may contain individual entry numbers corresponding to one or more of the aforementioned prize levels. To determine the Winners, individual entry numbers will first be compared with the winning numbers preselected by computer. For winning numbers not returned, prizes will be awarded in random drawings from among all eligible entries received. Prize choices may be offered at various levels. If a winner chooses an automobile prize, all license and registration fees, taxes, destination charges, and other expenses not offered herein are the responsibility of the winner. If a winner chooses a trip, travel must be complete within one year from the time the prize is awarded. Minors must be accompanied by an adult. Travel companion(s) must also sign release of liability. Trips are subject to space and departure availability. Certain black-out dates may apply.

The following applies to the sweepstakes named above:

No purchase necessary. You can also enter the sweepstakes by sending your name and address to: P.O. Box 508, Gibbstown, N.J. 08027. Mail each entry separately. Sweepstakes begins 6/1/93. Entries must be received by 12/30/94. Not responsible for lost, late, damaged, misdirected, illegible or postage due mail. Mechanically reproduced entries are not eligible. All entries become property of the sponsor and will not be returned.

Prize Selection/Validations: Selection of winners will be conducted no later than 5:00 PM on January 28, 1995, by an independent judging organization whose decisions are final. Random drawings will be held at 1211 Avenue of the Americas, New York, N.Y. 10036. Entrants need not be present to win. Odds of winning are determined by total number of entries received. Circulation of this sweepstakes is estimated not to exceed 200 million. All prizes are guaranteed to be awarded and delivered to winners. Winners will be notified by mail and may be required to complete an affidavit of eligibility and release of liability which must be returned within 14 days of date on notification or alternate winners will be selected in a random drawing. Any prize notification letter or any prize returned to a participating sponsor, Bantam Doubleday Dell Publishing Group, Inc., its participating divisions or subsidiaries, or the independent judging organization as undeliverable will be awarded to an alternate winner. Prizes are not transferable. No substitution for prizes except as offered or as may be necessary due to unavailability, in which case a prize of equal or greater value will be awarded. Prizes will be awarded approximately 90 days after the drawing. All taxes are the sole responsibility of the winners. Entry constitutes permission (except where prohibited by law) to use winners' names, hometowns, and likenesses for publicity purposes without further or other compensation. Prizes won by minors will be awarded in the name of parent or legal guardian.

Participation: Sweepstakes open to residents of the United States and Canada, except for the province of Quebec. Sweepstakes sponsored by Bantam Doubleday Dell Publishing Group, Inc., (BDD), 1540 Broadway, New York, NY 10036. Versions of this sweepstakes with different graphics and prize choices will be offered in conjunction with various solicitations or promotions by different subsidiaries and divisions of BDD. Where applicable, winners will have their choice of any prize offered at level won. Employees of BDD, its divisions, subsidiaries, advertising agencies, independent judging organization, and their immediate family members are not eligible.

Canadian residents, in order to win, must first correctly answer a time limited arithmetical skill testing question. Void in Puerto Rico, Quebec and wherever prohibited or restricted by law. Subject to all federal, state, local and provincial laws and regulations. For a list of major prize winners (available after 1/29/95): send a self-addressed, stamped envelope entirely separate from your entry to: Sweepstakes Winners, P.O. Box 517, Gibbstown, NJ 08027. Requests must be received by 12/30/94. DO NOT SEND ANY OTHER CORRESPONDENCE TO THIS P.O. BOX.

Bestselling Women's Fiction

Sandra Brown

_____	28951-9 TEXAS! LUCKY	$5.99/6.99 in Canada
_____	28990-X TEXAS! CHASE	$5.99/6.99
_____	29500-4 TEXAS! SAGE	$5.99/6.99
_____	29085-1 22 INDIGO PLACE	$5.99/6.99
_____	29783-X A WHOLE NEW LIGHT	$5.99/6.99
_____	56045-X TEMPERATURES RISING	$5.99/6.99
_____	56274-6 FANTA C	$4.99/5.99
_____	56278-9 LONG TIME COMING	$4.99/5.99

Amanda Quick

_____	28354-5 SEDUCTION	$5.99/6.99
_____	28932-2 SCANDAL	$5.99/6.99
_____	28594-7 SURRENDER	$5.99/6.99
_____	29325-7 RENDEZVOUS	$5.99/6.99
_____	29316-8 RECKLESS	$5.99/6.99
_____	29316-8 RAVISHED	$4.99/5.99
_____	29317-6 DANGEROUS	$5.99/6.99
_____	56506-0 DECEPTION	$5.99/7.50

Nora Roberts

_____	29078-9 GENUINE LIES	$5.99/6.99
_____	28578-5 PUBLIC SECRETS	$5.99/6.99
_____	26461-3 HOT ICE	$5.99/6.99
_____	26574-1 SACRED SINS	$5.99/6.99
_____	27859-2 SWEET REVENGE	$5.99/6.99
_____	27283-7 BRAZEN VIRTUE	$5.99/6.99
_____	29597-7 CARNAL INNOCENCE	$5.50/6.50
_____	29490-3 DIVINE EVIL	$5.99/6.99

Iris Johansen

_____	29871-2 LAST BRIDGE HOME	$4.50/5.50
_____	29604-3 THE GOLDEN BARBARIAN	$4.99/5.99
_____	29244-7 REAP THE WIND	$4.99/5.99
_____	29032-0 STORM WINDS	$4.99/5.99
_____	28855-5 THE WIND DANCER	$4.95/5.95
_____	29968-9 THE TIGER PRINCE	$5.50/6.50
_____	29944-1 THE MAGNIFICENT ROGUE	$5.99/6.99
_____	29945-X BELOVED SCOUNDREL	$5.99/6.99

Ask for these titles at your bookstore or use this page to order.

Please send me the books I have checked above. I am enclosing $ _____ (add $2.50 to cover postage and handling). Send check or money order, no cash or C. O. D.'s please.

Mr./ Ms. _____

Address _____

City/ State/ Zip _____

Send order to: Bantam Books, Dept. FN 16, 2451 S. Wolf Road, Des Plaines, IL 60018

Please allow four to six weeks for delivery.

Prices and availability subject to change without notice.

FN 16 - 4/94